TEMPTATION ON THE ALPINE EXPRESS

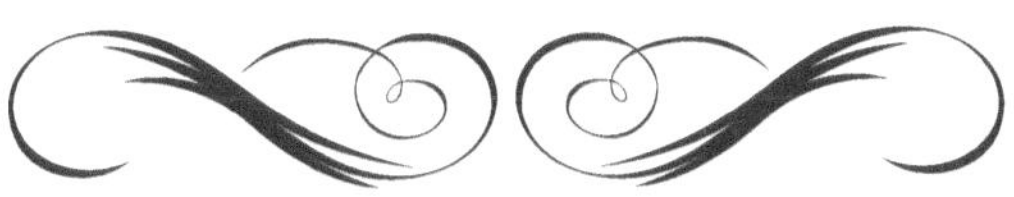

KIRSTEN S. BLACKETER

DEDICATION

Thanks, Niki. You gave me the spark of inspiration I needed to bring Nikolai Veronia to life. Armie Hammer and his Russian accent added fuel to the fire.

To all those secondary characters, you'll get your chance.

Don't be so demanding.

Dear Reader,

Welcome and thank you for selecting Temptation on the Alpine Express for your reading pleasure. I truly hope you enjoy the story and fall in love with the characters.

My motto as a historical romance author has always been: If I can't be completely historically accurate, then I will at least make it historically feasible. On that note, I beg a few indulgences in the accuracy of all my stories. My love has always been for the characters first and then the setting. I use the second only to enhance the first.

I did research on the Orient Express and the Russian empire for this story and took some creative liberties. Forgive me. I tried to interfere as little as possible while still keeping it feasible.

Enjoy the adventure and the romance, let it whisk you away if only for a short time. We all need a little escape sometimes.

Sending warm regards and best wishes your way. Remember to be kind and love one another.

With best wishes and love,

Kirsten S. Blacketer

TABLE OF CONTENTS

Chapter One   1

Chapter Two   7

Chapter Three   19

Chapter Four   31

Chapter Five   44

Chapter Six   56

Chapter Seven   66

Chapter Eight   77

Chapter Nine   89

Chapter Ten   98

Chapter Eleven   111

Chapter Twelve   125

Chapter Thirteen   137

Chapter Fourteen   150

Epilogue   156

Chapter One

June 1894
Vienna, Austria

The gilded white door towered before her. A shaft of afternoon sunlight reflected off the gigantic, ornate brass knocker inset with the head of a dragon. Gertrude Bleul swallowed the lump in her throat. This job would give her the fresh start she desperately needed. Ignoring the twist of conscience prodding at the back of her mind in warning, she announced her presence with two echoing thuds of the intimidating knocker against the massive door.

Several seconds passed until the doors opened like a gaping maw threatening to swallow her whole. A butler, wearing a powdered white wig, appeared in the doorway. His impassive expression remained fixed as his gaze drifted over her.

"Good day. I have an appointment with Countess von Breunner. I believe I am expected." Gertrude quelled the butterflies in her stomach as he stepped aside and gestured for her to enter.

"This way, madam." He closed the door behind her with a solid thud and escorted her through the opulent entryway lined with golden trim and expensive tapestries. Her worn heels clicked on the pristine marble floors and echoed off the vaulted ceiling.

Gertrude cleared her throat and focused on remaining calm. The first impression was always the most important. The mantra repeated in her mind. She clutched her handbag with both hands as though prepared to fend off an attack should it arise.

The butler stopped and opened a door off the main entryway.

Inside, Gertrude nearly stumbled over the edge of the thick Persian carpet. Soft hues of red, blue, and gold touched every surface. The delicate lighting enriched the comfort of the room lending a warmth to the plush cushions and vivid, jewel toned art hanging on the wall. Warm and inviting, her new surroundings contrasted with the rest of the house she left behind.

"*Guten tag, Frauelin Bleul.* Please, come in. Sit down."

The rich, cultured, feminine voice caught Gertrude by surprise. She spun around to find the countess sitting on the red velveteen sofa with a black fur blanket draped across her lap. Her midnight-blue satin gown bore silver embroidery across the bosom and up over the right shoulder. The stitching resembled tiny birds captured in flight against a moonlit sky. Diamonds shimmered against her throat and around her wrists. A single, bold gem adorned the ring finger of her left hand, glinting when she moved.

"Your Grace." Gertrude dropped into a curtsey, lowering her gaze to the carpet. The woman before her looked not a day over forty, and yet she knew the countess to be much closer to her mid-fifties. The countess's blue eyes sparkled with intelligence and youth. Her silver hair pulled loosely into a simple, yet elegant style, gave the only true indication of her age. This refined elegance put her at odds with what Gertrude expected and left her pleasantly surprised.

"Do you like my little oasis?" the countess asked, gesturing to the room with a diamond studded wave of her hand.

"It is lovely, Your Grace." She straightened her posture, but ensured her gaze remain subdued.

"Sit down." The countess gestured to the seat opposite her. "Serve the tea, if you please."

With a nod, Gertrude sat and placed her bag beside her before preparing the tea laid neatly on the table between them. This was a request she could perform with her eyes closed. Without hesitation, she set to her task.

"How do you take your tea, Your Grace?" she asked as she poured the hot liquid into the cups.

"One sugar, no cream."

Gertrude offered the cup and saucer then resumed her seat. She met the countess's gaze and folded her hands in her lap.

"You may make yourself a cup, if you wish." The countess smiled before taking a sip.

With the same quick efficiency, Gertrude prepared herself a cup of tea and savored the rich, exotic flavor warming her down to her very soul.

"Delicious, is it not? I have it imported from the East." The countess set aside her tea and stroked the fur blanket across her lap. A pair of green eyes peered up at Gertrude from the mass of black fur.

Gertrude jumped nearly upsetting her tea. She set the saucer aside and pressed a hand to her heart. "Is that a cat?"

The countess chuckled. "It is." She scratched under the beast's chin, and it rubbed against her glittering hand. "His name is Luca." The animal turned his emerald eyes toward her, his gaze unflinching as he settled his head down on his mistress' lap once more.

"He is quite handsome." Gertrude cleared her throat. "Forgive me, I mistook him for a blanket. Gave me quite a start."

The countess's laughter filled the room. "He is quite beastly. Aren't you, my pet?" She scratched his head and then turned her attention back to Gertrude. Her sharp eyes flashed with amusement. "I must say, your papers are impeccable, my dear."

"Thank you, Your Grace." Her cheeks warmed under the scrutiny.

"Yes, your services come highly recommended."

"I am honored you approve, Your Grace."

"There is one thing that puzzles me." The countess tapped her finger against her lip.

A knot twisted in Gertrude's stomach. Her heart threatened to cease beating. *Please, no.* She swallowed the bile burning the back of her throat.

"Why on earth would you leave such a wonderful employer?"

Gertrude dropped her gaze to her hands unable to maintain

the façade she spent so long cultivating. "I hoped to travel more, Your Grace. You are searching for a traveling companion as well as a ladies' maid." She lifted her gaze with certainty in her words. "I believe I can fill those requirements admirably."

The countess nodded, a smile playing upon her lips. "I agree. You seem spirited and willing to work. What languages do you speak?"

"German, French, and English, Your Grace."

"German is your native tongue?"

"Yes, Your Grace."

"Do you speak any Russian?"

Gertrude shook her head. "No, but if you require me to learn, I will do so."

"It is not necessary." The countess waved her hand. "You may begin immediately. Have your items delivered here. Nikolai can show you to your chambers."

A tall, broad figure separated from the shadows behind the countess. A man clothed entirely in black with dark hair and the deepest jade-colored eyes stood behind the sofa where the countess lounged.

Gertrude jumped, this time tipping her tea onto the carpet. She snatched up a towel and blotted the spot fervently. "My apologies." Her attention drifted from the carpet to the imposing man who materialized out of the air. His broad shoulders flexed as he leaned down to speak to the countess.

The shadow's gaze burned through her. He spoke in Russian. The heavily accented words wrapped in a deep timbre Gertrude felt in the depths of her soul. His chiseled jaw ticked as he studied her.

The countess replied in Russian before turning her attention back to Gertrude. "Oh, do not fuss over it. I shall have Ivan take care of it in a moment."

Gertrude placed the towel aside and rose to her feet. "Thank you, Your Grace."

"Dinner is at seven. Plenty of time to settle in. Nikolai will ensure you have everything you need." The countess smiled. Even Luca spared her a curious glance as she followed Nikolai out into the hallway. "I look forward to learning more about you, Gertrude."

The door closed behind them, leaving her in the company of the hulking Russian shadow.

Obediently, she followed, noting the rooms and the corridors they passed as they climbed the staircase to the third floor. Silence enhanced the ominous nature of the man leading her deeper into the ostentatious, palatial home.

They turned down a narrow corridor with rooms on either side. When Nikolai came to an abrupt stop, Gertrude collided with his solid back. He spun around and steadied her with one large hand. His intense gaze and stoic demeanor made him more intimidating than handsome, and yet somehow he still managed to steal her breath.

"Thank you," she mumbled, straightening to her full height.

He released the hold on her arm. The sweet scent of anise mixed with leather reached her nose.

"Are you always so clumsy?" His accented English betrayed his Russian heritage, and yet he showed no attempt to hide it or his contempt for her.

"I am not clumsy."

"You are worse than a newborn foal. Skittish and jumpy." His gaze narrowed. "What are you afraid of, *malen'kiy zherebenok*?"

Irritated at his use of words unfamiliar to her, Gertrude squared her shoulders, her shawl pulling tight around her. "I am not afraid of anything."

"Perhaps you should be." His eyes darkened to a deep stormy blue.

"What did you say? The Russian part." She forced herself to meet him with a boldness she did not feel and not shrink away. No matter how handsome or intimidating he appeared, he could do no worse than others had done.

His wolfish grin made her knees tremble. She forced her expression to remain impassive, but he made it so difficult. Nikolai transformed right before her eyes. Gone was the stoic shadow replaced by a rogue with terrifying charm.

Gertrude stepped back unable to trust her own reaction to him. "Who are you?"

Instantly, the grin dissipated. "Nikolai Voronia. I serve as a personal guard for the Countess von Breunner." He turned and opened the door to his right. "This is your room." Without another word, Nikolai pushed past her and retreated down the hallway in the direction they had come.

When he disappeared around the corner, Gertrude entered the room and closed the door behind her. Inside, she leaned against it and surveyed her new living space. Her heart pounded and her mind raced. What happened? What kind of man was Nikolai Voronia? One who could turn off the charm as easily as one could extinguish a flame?

She should be happy. Ecstatic even, since working for the countess would not only give her a fresh start but also an opportunity to explore the world. Instead of being able to rejoice in her new situation, she found herself torn.

Gertrude shivered at the memory of the handsome man whose eyes embodied both the warmth of a summer sky and the chill of an alpine winter. Whoever Nikolai Voronia was, he would certainly be a threat if she allowed him. That much was certain.

The solution was simple. She would not give him the opportunity. No matter how charming or intimidating, Nikolai would not be allowed to hold her life or her heart in his hand.

No man would. Never again.

CHAPTER TWO

November 14, 1899
Paris, France

The light from nearby windows spilled onto the street. Nikolai focused his attention on the parts which remained in shadow. The tall hedges lining the walking paths, the alleys cut through the homes every block or so. His gaze shifted back and forth scanning for anything out of place. Any possible threat to the family he swore to protect.

He shifted in his seat beside the driver. Inside the safety of the carriage behind him sat the countess and her companion. As tempting as it had been to accept the countess's invitation to join them inside the carriage, Nikolai maintained his decision to remain where he could better keep watch.

More importantly, it would keep him from being distracted by her. *Gertrude.* The countess's companion served his mistress faithfully for the past five years, and even though he had no reason to doubt her loyalty or sincerity, there was something about her which continually nagged at his conscience. Honestly, if he allowed himself the small concession, he found himself smitten with the fierce, blonde angel who challenged him on every occasion.

Nikolai's scowl deepened. The drifter shifted beside him uncomfortably.

"Something amiss, sir?" the driver asked, his voice trembling in the cold November air.

"No." Shaking the distracting thoughts from his mind, Nikolai scolded himself and returned his mind to the task at hand.

The driver gave the team a nudge, and they made rather

decent time to the countess's Parisian home. His mistress loved Paris, but she loathed travel. When they did venture to the heart of France, they often stayed for extended periods as to give her adequate time to recuperate from the tedium of the train journey.

Nikolai never dissuaded her. In fact, he rather preferred not to be in Vienna. Her husband, the count, proved an imbecile with more ego than intelligence who offered little substance to any conversation but thought quite highly of himself and his standing in Viennese society. Their marriage happened long before Nikolai came into her service, and while it had not been a love match, the power and influence of both their families brokered a business deal of sorts with their union. By the time Nikolai met the countess, she had several children and a penchant for knowing exactly what she wanted. Which is precisely how he arrived in her service ten years before.

The carriage drew to a halt in front of the stately home a few blocks from the Sine River. As he stepped down from the carriage, his sharp gaze shifted quickly over the nearby landscape. Several pedestrians ambled along the walk across the street. A cart rumbled past carrying a heavy load of coal. He rounded the carriage and opened the door, offering his hand. The countess stepped through first. Her crimson cloak shone blood red under the dim street lights.

"Thank you," she murmured in Russian.

Nikolai nodded and released her hand. When he turned back to the carriage, his gaze locked with Gertrude's. He offered his hand.

She hesitated for a half second before taking it. Every time he offered, she hesitated as though afraid his touch would taint her. Once her feet found solid ground, she relinquished his grip and followed the countess up the stairs.

Nikolai flexed his hand where the warmth of her touch branded him. He steeled himself and took one last sweep of the vicinity before entering the house after them and locking the door securely behind him.

The staff rushed forward to gather their outer garments.

"We shall retire to the study." The countess dismissed the

servants with a wave of her hand.

Gertrude stole a glance in his direction. She smoothed her hands over her silver apron which complimented the dark blue dirndl bodice she wore. The traditional Bavarian garment bridged the gap between servant and companion nicely, but it also served as a gentle reminder of her heritage, as if her lilting German accent did not accomplish this already. He cocked his head at her inquiring glance which only made her quickly divert her attention and follow the countess into the study.

His mouth twitched. Even after five years, she did not completely trust him. Well, after their tumultuous start, he could hardly blame her. It had not been his intention to terrify her upon their first meeting, but it must have left her wary of him. For every time he appeared, she gave a start. Skittish, like a foal, and nearly as adorable. To this day, she gave him wide berth, as though he would attack her and ravage her beyond salvation. The tempting thought had certainly crossed his mind.

Nikolai suppressed the hunger lying beneath the surface of his controlled façade. He dared not give any indication of his true thoughts. Gertrude deserved far better than the devil who lurked in the shadows concealing his questionable past.

Quietly, he slipped into the study and surveyed the room. Gertrude poured a brandy for the countess, ignoring him as he stepped around her and took a seat in the far corner of the room.

The countess accepted the glass with delight. "Thank you, darling. Won't you join me?"

"No, thank you." Gertrude demurred and sat on the sofa opposite.

"That was quite an evening." The countess gushed. "Oh, such an exquisite performance. Don't you agree, my dear?"

"Yes. I enjoyed it immensely." Gertrude nodded.

"What of you, Nikolai? Did you enjoy it?" The countess turned in his direction.

"I cannot say. I hardly noticed the performance. My mind was occupied with other things." His gaze lingered on Gertrude for a half second before he corrected himself. "You employ me to keep you safe, not enjoy the theatre."

The countess clucked her tongue and shook her head with a laugh. "While I appreciate your attention to my safety, I would hate for you to miss out on life's finer gifts."

"I live to serve, Your Grace," Nikolai responded with the practiced air of a diplomat.

A knock interrupted the conversation. Nikolai tensed as the door opens revealing the butler carrying a letter.

"What is it?" The countess sipped her brandy, gesturing for Gertrude to accept the proffered correspondence.

Nikolai relaxed, wishing he could enjoy a small splash of vodka.

"There's no letter. Only a photograph with an inscription on the back in Russian I believe." Gertrude handed the card to the countess.

The countess gasped, and Nikolai sprang to his feet instantly. Within a moment, he appeared by her side. "What is it?"

The countess's normally rosy cheeks were pale and drawn. "Gertrude, please fetch me my tonic, upstairs. Now!"

Gertrude startled at the countess's harsh tone but quickly darted from the room, leaving Nikolai alone with the countess.

She pressed her hand to her chest and leaned back against the couch.

"What is it?" Nikolai never saw the countess so affected by anything, let alone a small photograph. Perhaps it was something truly dire to cause her such distress.

The countess opened her eyes, fear and uncertainty hid in their vivid blue depths. Her lips trembled as though the words hesitated on the tip of her tongue. She pressed her mouth closed firmly and shook her head.

Nikolai took the photograph she held out in an unsteady hand. Several people stood at the center of the photograph. The edges frayed and the details of the image faded with time. But there was no mistaking the people in the photograph. The countess stood in the middle, beside her sister, along with two other men, approximately the same age. Behind them, stood several other people, whom Nikolai recognized instantly as members of the royal Russian family.

"This is you?" Nikolai pointed to the young woman in the front row.

The countess nodded. "Me and my sister. Our cousins here. And in the background, you see the rest of the royal household including the late Emperor."

"Why does this upset you?"

"Read the back." She gestured to the photograph.

In Russian the words, *We know the truth. Return, or he dies,* were written in flowing script.

As though a flame to tinder, Nikolai launched into action. "Who sent this? What does this mean? Is your son in danger?" He glanced at the photo once more and then at the words. Simple and direct, yet he could not make sense of them.

"I do not know who sent it." The countess inhaled deeply and rose to her feet. As she paced, she twisted the ring on her finger. "If I knew, I would have you hunt them down and demand answers."

"What truth are they speaking of?" Nikolai's mind spun quickly gears interlocking and connecting pieces of information. "Perhaps a secret you're hiding?"

The countess's derisive laugh made him pause. "With our status comes a great many secrets and a million lies. It could mean anything." She drew her lip between her teeth. The lines of worry set between her brows made the countess resemble her age.

"He dies?" Nikolai pondered aloud. "Who is he?"

"Who knows." She threw her hands up. "My idiotic husband. My son. My son-in-laws. It could be anyone."

"I have connections in Vienna who can help. Contacts in Russia, although those may take some time." He tapped the photograph in thought. "Perhaps we should return and sort it out."

The countess spun around to face him, her eyes sharp. "We've only just arrived. I cannot bear boarding a train again so soon." Her expression brightened. "You go back. Gertrude and I will follow next week."

Nikolai shook his head. "No. No, I cannot leave you here. Whoever sent this letter could be watching this house. Watching you. I will not leave you unprotected."

"I am capable of hiring someone while I am here. You can ensure I have the proper protection before you leave." She lifted her fingers to her lips and smiled. "Even better, what if I send you and Gertrude back to Vienna, with one of the maids posing as me. Since I never leave my compartment when I travel, no one will ever know."

The plan sounded utterly ridiculous. Nikolai folded his arms across his chest. "No one will believe it."

"Then you shall have to make it convincing." The countess snatched the photo from his hand. "Once you return to Vienna, find out who sent this and do what must be done to ensure my family's safety." Her eyes glittered with determination in the firelight.

Nikolai exhaled in irritation. "Something does not fit, and I do not like walking into a situation without knowing what to expect."

"Expect a war." The countess raised her chin high. "There are those who seek to crush what remain of the Russian royal lineage. They will not go down without a fight. Always be prepared for bloodshed."

His hand flexed at the word. It had been years since he had resorted to violence. He would do what needed to be done in order to secure the safety of the countess and her family. "Yes, Your Grace."

"Good. Book the next train to Vienna."

"We're leaving Paris so soon?" Gertrude's question brought Nikolai back from the darkness.

"Yes, dear. Come in, and I'll explain what is required of you."

Gertrude's curious cornflower gaze lingered on Nikolai as she crossed the room and handed the countess a teacup with her tonic in hot water. He felt the burn of her censure without a word crossing her beautiful lips.

"Nikolai, the train tickets," the countess reminded him.

"Yes." He took his leave as the countess explained her plan for them to return to Vienna while she remained in Paris.

He snatched his coat from the hall and tugged on his hat before stepping out into the cold once more. It barely affected him. After so many winters in St. Petersburg, he became impervious to cold. It had lost its ferocity.

As he made his way across the river to the station, the complexity of their charade took shape in his mind. Then he realized a small detail which set his soul on fire.

Gertrude would be by his side, and the knowledge pleased him more than it should.

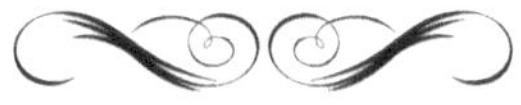

November 15, 1899

The morning sun had yet to rise and Gertrude found herself bundled in her warmest cloak riding in a carriage bound for the train station. She frowned. It had only been a few days since they arrived in Paris. She looked forward to their annual trip to the bustling metropolis which gave her a much-needed reprieve from Vienna.

The countess often took her as a traveling companion to Munich and Venice, but she found Paris to be the most diverting. Possibly because it was the furthest she had ever traveled from what she considered home.

Gertrude leaned against the door and pressed her cheek to the cool glass letting the carriage rock her. The ladies' maid who traveled with them, Julia, sat across from her bundled in the countess's rich velvet and wool cloak, her face shrouded with a veil. No one would believe, not even for a moment, that this maid was the countess.

Even after the countess explained the plan, Gertrude found herself at a loss. Why were they traveling back to Vienna? And why in heaven were they leaving the countess in Paris while using the maid as a decoy? Nothing made sense. The countess refused to give her any clear answers, merely asking her to have faith in her and Nikolai.

She exhaled sharply at the thought of the man who plagued her. For the last five years, he caused nothing but agitation and frustration. She found his company both infuriating and comforting. A combination which left her bereft and confused. Whatever plot he and the countess had devised, she was to play a central role, although neither provided her with any details. What was written on the back of the photograph? What did it mean? It obviously factored into this hasty return to Vienna.

Nikolai, however, proved as immovable as a mountain when she asked for clarification upon leaving the countess's Parisian home. He merely directed her to get into the carriage and remain silent. She folded her arms across her chest. Cold and infuriating as he was, she dared not disobey him. One thing she learned over the years, Nikolai served as protector not because he was intimidating, but because he was damned proficient in his abilities.

The carriage slowed to a halt in front of the train station. Several seconds later, Nikolai swung open the door and offered his hand. Gertrude nudged the maid posing as the countess who squeaked and rushed from the carriage. Gertrude followed behind, watching the two play the role assigned to them.

Nikolai instructed the porter to fetch their bags and led the imposter countess to her compartment.

Waiting a few steps behind, Gertrude allowed herself a moment to watch Nikolai work. His stoic demeanor and sharp gaze aligned with the authoritative tone of his voice. No one would dare question him. Her whole body warmed. He truly was a force to behold.

Once he situated the countess in her compartment, he reemerged into the hallway. Gertrude straightened in his presence, sensing he may find some fault with her posture or her lack of decorum. She was still expected to play the part of companion even though the true countess was not aboard the train.

"This is your compartment." Nikolai gestured to the room beside the countess's. "I will be in this one." He pointed to the one on the opposite side.

She opened the compartment and stepped inside, spinning around quickly when he followed her inside and closed the door.

"What are you doing?" She stepped back until her thighs hit the table by the window.

His gaze roamed the room twice before he faced her. "Ensuring the room is secure."

"Why in heaven's name would it not be secure?" She propped her hands on her hips. "We have just reserved these compartments last evening."

He raised his brow. "I had to hunt down the original occupants and acquire the compartments from them before finalizing the transfer with the company. The train was nearly full, and I required three compartments all in one car."

"Oh." Gertrude cleared her throat and turned toward the window facing the platform.

With a snap, the blinds fell into place blocking the outside from view. She spun to find Nikolai a breath away, his hand on the mechanism to lower the curtain. Her heart thundered in her chest at his proximity. The intoxicating scent of anise and leather surrounded him. She avoided being this close to him for precisely this reason. He distracted her with his voice, but most of all with his scent. He brought thoughts of spiced wine and forbidden pleasures to the forefront of her mind.

She stumbled back and caught her shin on the edge of the bed. "*Verdammt.*"

"Still so skittish." He clicked his tongue in distaste, his expression unyielding. "Five years and still you do not trust me."

"Why should I?" Gertrude rubbed her leg and scowled at him. "You've given me no reason to do so."

"Oh, I beg to differ." A wolfish smile curled his lips transforming him from protector to predator. "You will always be safe in my company."

"Says the fox to the hen," she muttered beneath her breath.

He smiled and her heart lurched with an aching need to reach for him. "One day you will have to trust me, *liebling.*"

Gertrude sucked in a breath at the word. Before this

moment, he never even uttered a German word. But this one stole her breath. *Darling.* A pet name. She shook her head, unwilling to think of the implications of such a pronouncement. He toyed with her. She steeled herself and gestured toward the door.

"I am quite safe. You may go."

"Knock if you require anything." He pointed to the wall beside the bed. Those bewitching eyes sparkled with amusement before turning to ice. Without another word, he retreated from her room leaving her alone with her thoughts.

Gertrude collapsed on the bed and stared at the ceiling. What in the devil? She could never make heads nor tails of her conversations with Nikolai. It always felt as if he were playing a complex game of chess with her emotions. One moment showing interest and the next disdain. She sighed. Why could she not confront him once and for all?

The man was no impressionable youth. In fact, he held nearly fifteen years seniority over her if her estimation was correct. Nikolai had once been part of the royal Russian guard at the Winter Palace in St. Petersburg. He served his country and abandoned life as a soldier to serve the countess. Whatever bits and pieces of information she garnered from the countess over the years only fed her curiosity. She dared not ask Nikolai directly. Though she knew he would never bring her harm, she could not bear the thought of his censure.

Yes, they argued like a pair of pernicious children on many occasions, but Gertrude longed for a deeper connection with the enigmatic protector. The secrets he guarded must be great indeed for him to seal himself in such a wall of ice and steel. Over the years, he showed no willingness to share his past with anyone, especially her. This brought her only frustration and sadness. How lonely an existence it must be for him to bear such secrets alone?

Gertrude sat up and cleared her throat. Did she not keep her own secrets buried deep inside, hidden from all those around her? She shook her head. This was not the time for such thoughts. Perhaps one day she would be able to bear her heart, but not today, and most assuredly not to Nikolai.

The train whistle echoed through the car making her jump. She pressed her hand to her heart. Perhaps she was too nervous. Once the train left the station, she would proceed to the dining car and enjoy some breakfast and tea.

A knock came from the compartment door.

"Yes?" she called out.

"I have your baggage, madame."

Gertrude opened the door. The porter brought her bag as well as the countess's into her room.

"The gentleman requested I leave the countess's luggage with you." He bowed and took the coin she offered.

"Thank you." She watched him retreat down the hall and then knocked on Nikolai's door.

It opened without hesitation.

His gaze narrowed on her. "Is there a problem?"

"Yes." Gertrude shoved her way past him and into his room. His suitcase lay open on his bed. When she turned, she noticed he wore only his white shirt unbuttoned enough to reveal a dusting of hair across his chest. All thoughts disintegrated in her mind at the sight of the white linen stretched tight across his shoulders as he crossed his arms over his chest.

He leaned against the door. "Well?"

"What are we doing here?" Gertrude flailed her arms to encompass the room.

"We are on a train bound for Vienna." His expression remained steadfast and unreadable.

"Yes, I know that. I mean why are we returning to Vienna without the countess? Why are we pretending the maid is the countess? What reason could we possibly have for such a charade?" Her eyes widened. "Unless you have reason to believe she is in danger."

His lip twitched. "Perhaps you should not concern yourself with the details. It would be best if you played the part asked of you and left the details to me."

"Do not treat me as though I am some incompetent child who needs to be reminded of her place." Gertrude jabbed a finger in his chest. "I may only be a servant, but I deserve to know if my life is in danger."

Nikolai's hand wrapped around hers. His fingertips brushing hers as his grip held steady. The sensation nearly uprooted her. Never before had he touched her in such a way. Always courteous and fleeting, but this intentional breach of boundaries breathed life into the wordless attraction simmering between them for years.

"I would never put you in harm's way." His eyes glinted in the lantern light. "Never."

The thundering of her heart must have been audible because he drew her closer making it beat even faster. Gertrude licked her lips and tipped her chin back to meet his intense gaze.

"Tell me. Please."

He shook his head.

She tried to jerk from his hold. He held her tighter.

"Trust me, *liebling*." He softened his hold. "It is better if you do not know the details."

Gertrude sighed, and he released her hand. "Very well."

He offered a half smile and stepped aside to open the door.

She paused in the doorway. "I shall be in the dining car once we leave the station." Without waiting for his permission, she returned to her room and closed the door.

Her heart beat a rapid flutter against her chest, like a caged bird begging to take flight. She rested her hand over her chest and inhaled deeply. One of these days, the enigmatic Nikolai Voronia would be her downfall, and even with this knowledge, she welcomed her own demise with open arms.

CHAPTER THREE

The last person Nikolai expected to see on the Alpine Express from Paris to Vienna was Major Anson Montgomery. While he considered the gentleman to be a friend of sorts, the entirety of their acquaintance lay deep beneath murky waters fraught with secrets and lies. Nothing personal, of course, purely political. In fact, Nikolai quite enjoyed Anson's company. They were cut of the same cloth and worked in similar circles amid Viennese high society.

But their unlikely bond began long before Viennese politics and social graces. A much more complicated time and events best left in the past.

The moment Nikolai spotted Anson in the lounge, he swore beneath his breath. Was it not complicated enough to enact a charade in which he was the only one who knew of the dire consequences pending its failure?

He contemplated the circumstances of the last few days and wondered if Anson had been following them. Nikolai grinned knowing he could verify his assertion easily. Anson possessed a penchant for chronicling his interactions in leatherbound notebook he kept tucked inside the breast pocket of his coat. He often saw Anson absently touch the pocket as though ensuring it remained safely out of sight. If Anson had come to Paris solely to collect information on himself or the countess, Nikolai would discover the truth of it. Whether from Anson's own lips or from the notebook would yet be determined.

Interestingly, Anson seemed as surprised at Nikolai's presence as he had been upon seeing an old friend in such an inauspicious meeting place. Was it truly so unlikely for them to cross paths? It seemed so, but even he had to admit, the world became smaller with every passing year thanks to innovation and technology.

Anson changed little from one encounter to another. The patriotic Brit he once saved sat nursing a glass of scotch at the ungodly hour most were still abed. *Interesting.*

Nikolai entered the lounge without a sound, slipped a flask of vodka from his pocket, and poured some in a clean glass sitting on the bar.

"What is this you are drinking at such an hour?"

Anson spun around at his question. "I thought you of all people would understand the need for a drink before sunrise."

Nikolai sat in the chair across from him and raised his glass in salute.

Anson did the same, looking downright lost and finishing the contents in one swallow. His mouth twisted in a grimace.

Nikolai smirked, haphazardly hiding it behind the glass. "Scotch does not agree with you, my friend. Perhaps you should stick to the vodka."

"I wish it were as simple as that." He stared out the window at the sun rising over the horizon. After a pensive moment, he turned back, his gaze sharp. "Traveling with the countess?"

Nikolai nodded, knowing Anson was nothing short of thorough and attentive. "And her maid. She pays me well to ensure her safety when traveling through Europe. Since the incident in Moscow with her son, she has grown paranoid." He paused not wanting to overplay his hand. "For good reason."

He left the details vague, intent on keeping the focus of the conversation on Anson and not on himself. The less he offered, the less Anson pried. This was the unspoken agreement of their friendship.

"Tension is growing across Europe, Nikolai. There is no stopping it." Anson's gaze settled on his glass, seemingly distracted by a memory, before it met his once more. "The countess is fortunate to have your protection."

"This is true." Nikolai shrugged shifting the conversation once again. "What brought you to Paris?"

"Business with the consulate." Anson's vague reply belied the importance of the unspoken words when he pressed his hand to his breast pocket.

"Did things not go well?"

"Perfectly. Why do you ask?" Anson set his glass aside.

"Something troubles you, my friend. If not business, then it must be pleasure. A woman, perhaps?" he teased, sensing the uncharacteristic agitation brewing inside Anson.

"Must you always be so observant, Nikolai?"

"It is my gift. Not being so would make me inept, and the countess would not entrust me with her protection." He inclined his head and grinned knowing he broached a delicate subject. Very interesting indeed. "It is a woman. Who is this enchanting creature who stole your frigid heart?"

"For such a calculating individual, you harbor the heart of a romantic."

"Did you meet her in Paris?"

"It is complicated." Anson raked his hand through his hair.

"But you saw her while in the city, did you not?"

"Yes."

Nikolai waited patiently for Anson to continue. Silence made people uncomfortable. They rushed to fill the void with idle chatter spilling ubiquitous details without realizing it. Normally this tactic did not work on Anson, and yet he noted the agitation brewing beneath his friend's usually calm persona and decided to use it to his advantage.

"We dined last evening. It had been a long time since I last saw her, and the event left me certain she would enjoy her life much more without my being a part of it."

"You left her?"

Anson nodded. "She deserves better."

"I have heard that excuse before." Nikolai's own silent admonishment soured in his mind.

"It is the truth."

The carriage door opened with a whoosh of air. Both men turned toward the sound.

A lovely young woman shroud in black with a teasing hint of auburn curls stood in the doorway. Her gaze drifted over the occupants of the car before resting on Anson. Pink blossomed across her cheeks. She redirected her focus and strode across the lounge without a word. When she reached the door to the dining car, she exited without acknowledging their presence.

Nikolai caught the pained expression of frustrated longing painted on his friend's face. "Her?"

"Yes." Anson's hand clenched into a fist, his jaw set, gaze drifting back to the last place she had been.

"You do not seem surprised to see her."

"Why else would I be drinking scotch at dawn?"

"A valid point." Nikolai possessed all the information he required. Anson most certainly did not follow him to Paris. And this revealing turn of events left Nikolai more than slightly amused. Perhaps he could use Anson's predicament to his advantage. At least it would keep any suspicions of their hasty return to Vienna quelled during the trip. He only hoped the maid would remain in the compartment as she had been instructed.

"I am in compartment eight if you need something stronger to drink." He glanced through the window into the dining car catching a glimpse of Anson's lady accepting an invitation to join Gertrude. Nikolai whistled low, intent on stoking the flame. "But you should fix things, my friend, before someone steals her away."

He marked Gertrude's glowing smile and could almost hear her tinkling laughter. His heart clenched in his chest. If only he could coax such a reaction from her. Nikolai shook his head and retreated from the lounge.

When he reached his compartment, he braced his hands on the rack above the bed and took several deep breaths in a desperate moment to collect himself. When had these feelings intensified so dramatically?

This affinity for Gertrude was nothing new. Those feelings existed from the first moment he met her. And yet it caused him little effort to hide them away for both their sakes. Seeing Anson so affected must have broken something loose in himself, for now he found he longed for nothing but to commandeer her company all for himself.

To add fuel to the raging fire, he wondered at Gertrude's

ability to play her part in their charade. No one must uncover the truth. He must return to Vienna and discover who sent the photograph. Nikolai's sole mission was to protect the countess and her family. Nothing trumped his duty. Not even the deepest desire of his heart.

Pushing aside his inability to reconcile these dualities waging a battle inside of him, Nikolai took a deep breath and retreated to the corridor. He knocked on the countess's compartment door.

"Yes." A timid voice echoed through it. "Who is it?"

"Nikolai, Your Grace."

The door opened a crack and a large pair of hazel eyes peered up at him. Nikolai pushed open the door and quickly closed it behind him.

Frightened, the maid scuttled back pulling her robe tightly around her.

"You will never convince anyone you are a countess if you sound like a mouse." Nikolai folded his arms across his chest. "Speak loud and clear. Be confident. Demanding even. Give them no reason to challenge your authority."

"I apologize, sir." She dipped in a curtsey.

"Enough of that. For the duration of the time on this train, you are by all accounts Countess von Breunner. No one will question it if you maintain the illusion." He squared his shoulders. "Now. You shall open the door for no one but myself or Gertrude, is that understood?"

Her head bobbed furiously. "Yes, sir."

Nikolai rolled his eyes and prayed for strength. "One of us will bring your meals. Your compartment has private lavatory facilities. If you require anything further, let us know."

"Of course, sir."

"Very well. Remain in this room." Nikolai left her and ensured the lock clicked into place before retreating down the corridor. He could ensure the maid's cooperation, if only through pure intimidation. The poor girl looked about ready to cry when he demanded she show some confidence. He exhaled sharply.

Gertrude proved to be far more complicated, and not only because of his feelings for her. Lately she endeavored to push beyond what he would consider acceptable behavior. She constantly challenged him, butting against his authority, pushing back in defiance. But he had never been able to fully trust her, although he wanted to, desperately.

When he returned, he noted Anson watching from the far corner while Gertrude and the young woman in black conversed amicably. He noted the other patrons in the carriage. A pair of young bucks who seemed vaguely familiar, an older gentleman with glasses reading a book near the window, and a middle-aged couple who seemed more engrossed in their own conversation than anyone else's presence around them.

"Good morning, ladies. I hope I am not interrupting." Nikolai smiled at Gertrude's obvious irritation at his uninvited presence. "Allow me to introduce myself. Mr. Nikolai Voronia, at your service, madam." He proffered a small bow.

Her bright green eyes widened. "Oh, how delightful. I am Mrs. Hudson." Her smile sparkled. "I apologize if this seems forward, but your accent. Is it Russian?"

"You have a good ear." He grinned turning on the charm. "Yes, I spent most of my life in St. Petersburg."

"How exciting!" She clapped her hands together.

Gertrude's silence spoke clearly.

"If you will excuse us, the countess has requested Gertrude's assistance." Nikolai pulled out Gertrude's chair and together they bade goodbye to the object of Anson's affection before leaving the dining car.

Once they reached the door to his compartment, she rounded on him. "Must you ruin everything?"

Nikolai grabbed her arm and pulled her into his compartment, slamming the door. "I ruined nothing. You had your little socialization and made a new acquaintance, but do not forget for a moment, we must be vigilant."

"Vigilant for what?" Gertrude propped her hands on her hips. "You have told me nothing. All I know is we are pretending to escort the countess back to Vienna. Nothing about this plan makes sense, Nikolai. Nothing."

"You know what you need to know. Just do as you have been told." He leaned against the door and admired the way her chest rose and fell with the exertion of her exaggerated breaths.

"Do you truly think I am incapable of following these simple instructions?" Her blue stare pinned him in place.

"No. But I cannot take the chance of you accidentally saying something suspicious to this new friend. Especially when she is tied to Anson." The last sentence was more for himself, but she snatched it up quickly.

"I would never betray a confidence." She bristled with indignation and arched her brow. "Who is Anson? The man with Matilda...I mean, Mrs. Hudson?"

"Yes."

"Is he a friend of yours?" Her eyes glittered at this new information.

"We know each other. It is complicated."

"Everything is complicated with you, Nikolai." Gertrude sighed. "You do not have to worry about me. I will see if the countess would like breakfast."

Nikolai stepped aside. Alone with his thoughts once more, Nikolai raked his hand over his face.

"Yes, Gertrude. Complicated is an understatement."

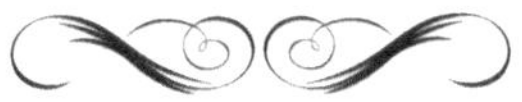

Later in the afternoon, against her better judgement, Gertrude agreed to luncheon with Nikolai. The silence stretched between them until Nikolai's attention shifted and a familiar voice broke the tension.

Nikolai smiled, a wholly unfamiliar and startling image in her mind, and rose from his seat to greet the new arrival.

"Please, sit down, Mrs. Hudson. My companion is quite exhausted of my company." Nikolai stepped aside and gestured to his seat, shifting his attention to Matilda's companion.

Gertrude studied the profile of the gentleman she assumed to be Anson. He bore a strong jawline and dark hair shaded with gray at the temples highlighted his handsome blue eyes. A striking gentleman to be sure. Together, he and Nikolai made quite a formidable pair.

"A word, Nikolai." Matilda's gentleman whisked him to a table in the far corner of the dining car.

The tension eased from Gertrude's shoulders. At least she would not have to endure Nikolai's silent judgement while she ate. Her interest in this blossoming relationship with Matilda drew her in. Even though they were new acquaintances, Gertrude felt a kinship to the woman across from her. She saw her own reflection deep beneath the surface. Perhaps this young woman could find happiness, unlike herself burdened with a haunted past and an unrequited desire lingering over her like a thundercloud.

"Come, I have only just ordered my food." Gertrude summoned the waiter, and Matilda ordered tea and soup.

Matilda fidgeted with the cloth napkin between her fingertips.

"Is something troubling you?" Gertrude asked.

The poor girl launched into an explanation of her history with Major Montgomery and her affection for the gentleman. She spoke of her confession of love and his brusque dismissal. Overwhelmed by the outpouring of honesty and trust by the young woman, Gertrude's heart ached for her. The poor darling truly had been crippled by cupid's arrow.

She listened intently, pausing only to interject a question or offer words of understanding. When Matilda's emotional tale came to an end, Gertrude sipped her tea and pondered the situation thoughtfully.

"I am at a loss. Perhaps I should admit defeat and return home. It is obvious the affection he has for me is not the same as what I hold for him." The girl's shoulder's slumped in defeat.

"I would not discount it yet, *liebling*." Gertrude's gaze drifted to where Nikolai sat, noting the major's attention continually centered on Matilda. "If I might make an observation?"

"Of course. I am desperate for advice."

"It seems the major is also trapped in a deep internal

struggle. You are young, *liebling*. He may wish to protect you in his own way. Perhaps he believes you deserve a love as youthful and full of optimism as you are."

Matilda shook her head. "I have tried to find love elsewhere, but no man can compare with the major. I love him."

"I understand." Gertrude rested her hand on Matilda's. "Would your parents approve of your choice of husband?" She refused to allow her mind to wander to a similar question asked of herself long ago.

"I do not know. Papa and the major were friends since before I was born. I would hope my father would understand and wish us every happiness."

"Does it concern you he may not condone such a union?"

"The thought never came into my mind. But after receiving such a forceful rejection from the major, yes, I am concerned my parents may overreact at the prospect of the major and I being together."

"I too know what it is like to pine for something forbidden." Longing pulled her under the waves of regret as her gaze met Nikolai's across the carriage. She shook her head and forced a smile for her gregarious companion.

"If you truly wish to capture his heart completely, then he must see the light you bring into his life. Let him see the lovely woman you have become. With a man such as the major, perhaps emphasizing your strengths and displaying your maturity will cause him to reevaluate his position." Perhaps if she were daring, she would heed her own advice. "Make no mistake, the man harbors emotions for you whether he admits them or not." The parallel of Matilda's situation to her own internal struggle was not lost on her.

"How can you possibly know with such certainty?"

"I am well past my prime, *liebling*, but I am not blind. He loves you. You need him to seize the opportunity placed before him, or he will lose you forever." The thought of losing her own opportunity with Nikolai stole her breath. Could she really offer such advice when she was clearly unable to do the same?

"Mr. Voronia?"

His name startled her for a moment, but Gertrude recovered quickly and conceded. "Yes, but there are other factors which are not so easy to overcome as yours." She shook off the sadness. "Never mind that. It shall come to right at some point."

Gertrude steered the conversation into lighter topics such as embroidery techniques and their mutual love of gothic literature.

While Nikolai seemed to hold suspicion for young Matilda, her company proved refreshing and provided a much needed distraction from the uncertainty of her own journey and this unending tension with the man who tormented her for so long.

Matilda's innocence revived Gertrude's trust in humanity. The uncertainty of not knowing if one's love is reciprocated can be the path toward utter madness. However, she knew Nikolai harbored no affection for her, since he chose to unleash his sarcastic wit and caustic tongue upon her at every possible opportunity. Perhaps a romance between them was doomed from the beginning.

Gertrude collected her bag from under the chair and excused herself to tend to the countess, determined to keep up the pretense or suffer Nikolai's wrath should their charade be uncovered. The waning sunlight outside flickered as the train wove through the French countryside toward Switzerland. When she passed his train compartment, she paused.

The door sat ajar. How strange.

She knew Nikolai remained in the dining car conversing with two gentlemen who were traveling together. He would never leave the door open, unless in their haste earlier, he forgot to close it properly.

With a glance down the corridor, she opened his compartment and slipped inside. His scent clung to the room. She brushed her fingers over his great coat hanging on the wall behind the door. After five years of working side-by-side for the countess, she memorized everything about him. From the exact shade of his eyes to the spicy masculine scent which belonged to him alone. It was branded upon her soul.

His suitcase sat in the rack above the bed. A small toiletry bag lay upon the table in front of the window. She peered inside, curious as to what cologne he used or if it were a soap.

"What are you doing in my room?"

Gertrude jumped and threw her bag in the air. It landed with a bang on the table beside his belongings. She pressed her hand to her chest and spun around, gripping the table for support.

"Nikolai, I..."

"Do not lie to me, Gertrude." His eyes blazed with intensity. "How did you get in here?"

The words refused to cross her dry lips. She licked them and cleared her throat. "I...the door was open when I passed by."

His gaze narrowed. "Tell the truth, or I will lock you in your compartment for the duration of this journey."

"You would punish me for something I did not do?" She crossed the distance between them and jabbed a finger in his chest. "The door was open."

"Do not make me put you over my knee." His voice rumbled beneath her touch.

The threat, as juvenile as it was, struck a deep, dark need inside her. "You do not scare me, Nikolai Voronia."

He snatched her wrist and pulled her so close their bodies were a breath from contact. "*Liebling*, when will you learn, you cannot lie to me."

She trembled beneath his touch, but not from fear. "You claim to know my mind better than I do?"

"I know many things about you." He released her wrist and stepped around her. "Did you touch anything in this room?"

"No." Gertrude gritted her teeth against his tone. Her heart pounded from the contact of his hand against her bare wrist. The scent of him surrounded her. She needed air, to be away from him, before she did something irrevocable. After one step toward the door, his voice rumbled behind her.

"Stay in your room tonight. Lock the door. Do not come out."

She glared at him over her shoulder and bit back the choice German words lingering on her tongue. Ones he would understand only by the tone of her voice. She retreated to her compartment and locked the door behind her.

Gertrude collapsed on the bed and buried her face in the pillow. Why was it always so complicated with him?

All the bravado and advice she gave Matilda earlier disintegrated into dust, and she could not help but wonder if there were truly any hope for her.

Nikolai hated her. Teasing her with his use of a sweet German endearment. Tormenting her with his voice. His scent. His very presence.

"*Mein Gott in Himmel,*" she muttered to the empty room. Perhaps it would be better if she found another place of employment. In the beginning, she convinced herself this fascination with the insufferable Russian would pass. But it only intensified.

She rubbed her wrist where his touch lingered like a haunting melody echoing down a vast corridor. If only she had the courage to tell him, or show him, what he did to her. How he drove her mad with longing and frustration.

But he could never know because deep in the pit of her gut she knew he did not share the same feelings for her as she harbored for him. Wallowing in despair, Gertrude collapsed on the bed and buried her face in the pillow.

She crossed a line, and Nikolai was far from forgiving. The ache in her heart comforted her until she fell asleep.

Chapter Four

If Gertrude was telling the truth, then someone broke into his compartment. But why? They would find nothing in his suitcase. If he carried anything of consequence, he retained it on his person. This was one of the first lessons he learned in the military, and the habit persisted as an agent in the Okhrana.

Nikolai searched the whole compartment and found nothing out of place, nothing missing. The sweet, cloying scent of Gertrude's soap hung in the air long after she left. The subtle touch of lemon verbena and rose water constantly reminded him of how close she was and punctuated every reason why he could not possess her.

Did she lie? What reason would she have to keep the truth from him? He pulled the flask of vodka from his pocket and poured some in a glass. Sitting on the edge of his bed, he sipped slowly while staring out the window barely noticing the passing scenery.

Silence fell on the room next door. Guilt settled in the vague vicinity of his heart and he sighed. Perhaps he had been too harsh in his reaction. But seeing her in his room, among his belongings, touching them as though reaching beyond their practical use as an extension of himself nearly undid him. Maybe it was wishful thinking which brought these thoughts to his mind.

No woman could ever see beyond the man he was, the things he did to survive, and still want him. Still love him. He shook the sentimental musings from his mind. Yes, he had taken lovers over the years, but not one touched his soul the way Gertrude did with her biting retorts and guarded personality.

But she did not want him. She would never be able to love him. Especially not if she knew the truth. He was a monster, and she deserved a man untarnished by the ghosts of his past.

His hand brushed his pocket. He reached inside and pulled out a leather journal. The worn edges showed years of loving attention. On the bottom the initial *M* stood out in gold embossing. It looked eerily similar to the one he had seen Anson carrying around in his pocket.

Only he knew exactly who this journal belonged to because he found it under her chair after she left the dining car earlier. He watched it fall out as she slid her bag from beneath the seat and tucked it under her arm. After he finished speaking with the two Italians, he snatched it up and slipped it into his pocket intent on returning it to her.

But when he found her in his room, returning the journal was the last thing on his mind.

During luncheon, he only half listened to Anson while they danced around the details of their true purpose in Paris. While Nikolai had been honest with their purpose in Paris, he purposely avoided discussing any details of their return to Vienna. He wished he could completely trust Anson. Even with their complicated history, they maintained a civil discourse while being entirely skeptical of the other's intentions. No matter the complicated relationship they shared, it worked, for the present at least.

Nikolai traced his fingertips over the soft leather journal. Would it hurt to open it? To read a few lines and see inside the mind of the woman who so fully captured his fantasies?

A burning curiosity threatened to consume him. Here in his hands lay the opportunity to see inside the mind of the one person he cared for more than any other. Dare he open it and reveal its secrets? Such an intimate, unforgivable action, diving between the pages of her journal without consent. What forbidden delights would he uncover?

He paused and frowned. What if it revealed his deepest fear? What he already believed to be the truth? She abhorred him. Could he truly weather such a revelation?

No. He set the journal beneath his pillow. He may be a monster, but he would not torment himself further.

Finishing his vodka, Nikolai ventured out into the corridor

in search of the porter. He would have their meals delivered to their compartments tonight. Perhaps they all needed some time to gather their thoughts and focus on the mission at hand. Besides, he could not have the poor maid impersonating the countess starve on her journey.

Realistically, he needed to maintain a closer account of his companion's whereabouts and keeping them confined seemed the most effective way to ensure their safety. He found the porter in the lounge car and requested their evening meals be delivered to his room.

Nikolai's gaze followed the porter as he entered the dining car. The two Italian gentlemen he spoke to briefly after luncheon remained at their table. From this vantage point he saw them perfectly through the glass window. Heads bowed together, they spoke, in Italian it seemed, as no one seemed particularly surprised by their animated conversation.

The few words he exchanged with them earlier solidified his assertion. He had seen them before. But where? Typically, Nikolai was able to pinpoint exactly where and when he had seen someone. His memory retained details like an iron trap. Where Anson carried his notebook to document his encounters, Nikolai relied solely on this unusual ability of retaining information with photographic precision.

However, the knowledge of where he previously encountered these two men evaded him completely. And that irritated him more than his persistent infatuation with Gertrude. Perhaps his age finally dulled the sharpness of his mind.

One of them glanced in his direction, Nikolai lifted his hand in salutation and turned away in an attempt to quell any question in their mind. But it did not matter, he knew, because he would bet any amount of coin these men knew who he was and it was only a matter of time before he uncovered their identities.

As he turned, he collided with the lone gentleman whom he had seen with a book earlier in the dining car.

"My apologies." He offered his hand. "Nikolai Voronia."

The bespeckled gentleman extended his own and spoke in a cultured French accent. "Oh, do not concern yourself. I should pay more attention to where I walk." He grinned and shook Nikolai's hand. "Dr. Phineas Archer, at your service."

Nikolai took a slow inventory of the gentleman before him. Slight build, graying brown hair, wire rimmed glasses, intelligent gray eyes, a bushy mustache, and well-worn tailored suit. In other words, the man fit the typical profile of others in his profession. He smiled in return. "So lovely to make your acquaintance, sir."

"And yours." The man beamed. "Are you traveling through to Vienna?"

"I am. And yourself?" Nikolai asked, his mind silently cataloguing every detail of the man before him.

"I am bound for Salzburg. A medical conference. Important progress to be made." He pushed his glasses up the bridge of his nose.

"Indeed. Must not stop progress."

"Are you bound for Russia by any chance?" the man asked.

Nikolai shook his head. "No. I have not seen my homeland in many years, unfortunately." He never took issue with his accent before and yet upon this journey it revealed much about him. Resentment and unease settled in the back of his mind.

"Ahhh, I see. I have heard of Russia's foreboding beauty. I dream of one day seeing it myself," Dr. Archer lamented. "What brings you aboard the Alpine Express?"

"I am traveling with the Countess von Breunner who is returning from Paris." He straightened his jacket. "If you will excuse me, I must ensure the countess has everything she requires."

"Oh, absolutely. Do not let me keep you." The gentleman stepped aside. "A pleasure to make your acquaintance, Mr. Voronia."

"Likewise." Nikolai bowed stiffly. "Good day." They departed in opposite directions.

As Nikolai walked down the corridor and crossed into the train car holding his compartment, his conversation with Dr. Archer replayed in his mind as did his earlier brief conversation with the two Italian men.

Inside his compartment, he sat on his bed and leaned back

against the wall. Perhaps his years of service made him too suspicious. Years of military training taught him to be suspicious and assume nothing. Everyone has an agenda which could be at odds with his mission. Even his current mission, ensuring the safety of the countess and her family.

Paranoia settled over him like a shroud. The sooner he arrived in Vienna and uncovered the identity of whomever sent the photograph to the countess, his mind would be at ease. Agitation flooded him. He longed to do something, anything, but there was no place to work off the nervous impatience pulsing beneath his flesh.

His thoughts drifted to Gertrude beyond the thin wall dividing them. No, he would not sully her with such thoughts or actions.

Instead, his gaze drifted to his pillow where her journal lay tucked beneath it. What harm would one glance do?

No. He should return it as a gentleman would. But Nikolai was no gentleman. He scoffed. One glance. Just a peek into the mind of the woman who drove him near to madness with desire. What would it hurt? No harm ever came from reading a book, especially the private journal of the countess's companion.

He smoothed his hands over the cover before opening it. Her sloping handwriting lay elegant against the fading pages. True to her character, it was written in her native tongue. While he had little occasion to speak German, he read it quite fluently. As he scanned the entry, it came to him slowly like peeling back the layers of a forgotten aged manuscript.

He noted the dates. This journal spanned many years, beginning nearly at the time of their first encounter five years ago. How interesting. It seemed she did not keep a daily log, but only wrote an entry when marking something of importance to remember.

The day they met remained engrained in his mind for eternity. Watching from the shadows, observing her posture and poise while meeting the countess for the first time, he gleaned volumes about her character from this encounter even if she did not know it. Excitement coursed through him at the thought of uncovering her thoughts of that day.

The first entry spoke of the countess and her new position. He scanned the entry until his name appeared in her bold script.

The countess employs a guardian of sorts. A tall, brutish man with a caustic tongue and little manners. I mistook him for a shadow at first and was startled by his presence.

Nikolai chuckled. Her description fit him perfectly. He could hardly fault her for such a first impression. He continued reading.

Handsome he may be, but it certainly does not atone for his horrible manners. He treated me with such indifference, I may as well have been a bit of mud caked on the bottom of his boot.

He frowned. Had he truly been so harsh?

He is a beast, and I doubt we shall ever be anything more than amicable enemies.

While it was not incorrect, it was unfortunate. Nikolai flipped through the pages until he found another entry bearing his name within the text.

Nikolai treats me with such contempt. I wonder if he will ever see me as more than merely an impediment to his work.

Now what could that possibly mean? He skipped ahead to an entry dated June 1896.

Tonight, I found myself in quite a state. Nikolai escorted the countess to a ball where I attended by her side. Forgive me for thinking such things. He creates such a conflict inside me, I know not whether to confess myself or hide my shame. There is one thing for certain, I cannot reveal my heart to him. For should he ever discover my thoughts of him, I would surely die of mortification.

Nikolai's eyes widened at the words. Could it be possible she harbored some affection for him? He read on.

I longed to feel his arms around me as he led me on the dance floor. How I love to dance. He is the only man who can ever fill the desire of my heart, but he can never know of my affection. He abhors my very presence. I feel his censure when he looks at me. How this knowledge pains me. The man I long for has no passion, no desire. He is carved of stone and I am nothing to him.

Unable to read more, he closed the journal and tucked it

back beneath his pillow. He stood and paced the floor of his small room wishing he could burst free from the confines. With a sigh he leaned his hand against the wall connecting his room to Gertrude's.

"Have I truly been so blind?" Nikolai groaned. Would it have changed anything if he had known the truth of her feelings for him? He shook his head.

There would never be anything between them because his life was not truly his own, and Gertrude deserved better than a bastard with no conscience and no home.

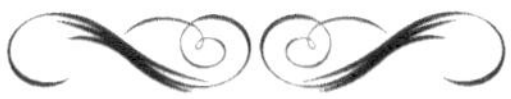

This journey proved more unenjoyable than any Gertrude had ever embarked upon. Between the expectation to maintain appearances of the countess's presence and her surly Russian traveling companion, she found it nearly impossible to maintain her sanity. An avalanche during the night merely extended the train's painfully slow progress. They spent hours awaiting the arrival of help to remove the snow blocking the tracks.

Fortunately, by breakfast, a team of men arrived from a nearby village, and with the aid of Nikolai, the major, and several other men aboard the train, they would certainly have the tracks cleared in no time.

Bless sweet Matilda for keeping her company and rescuing her from certain misery. The darling girl seemed tormented by her feelings for the major. Gertrude offered her own view of the matter, even though her own inability to face her own problems made her feel like a hypocrite. At least it kept their minds occupied.

"We cannot choose the ones we love." Gertrude took Matilda's hand.

"He told me I deserve better."

"You do." Matilda's eyes widened at the statement. "We both do." She squeezed the girl's hand offering both support and understanding.

"I still love him. I cannot help the way I feel."

"I understand, *liebling*." Deep in her heart, Gertrude understood all too well the ache of loving someone who seemed incapable of loving her in return.

Matilda shook her head. "The worst part of it all…when I injured my foot, and he rescued me."

Gertrude nodded, although her thoughts drifted toward Nikolai. Would he have come to her aid in such a manner?

"I thought I saw it." Matilda's voice softened. "The hunger in his gaze. It felt as though he wanted to kiss me and refrained. Perhaps I am imagining such things."

"If you saw the hunger there, why did you not act upon it?" The question spilled from her lips before she could stop it. Why would she encourage such behavior? *Because secretly, you want to do the same,* her conscience whispered.

"Why would I act upon it?"

"Did you want him to kiss you?"

"More than anything."

"Yet he did not."

"No." Matilda frowned. "But I want him to kiss me. How can I convince him to kiss me?"

Gertrude laughed at the absurdity of the question and yet she could not fault the logic behind it. "You cannot convince a man to do anything."

"Then what should I do?"

"Kiss him first." The answer came to her mind like a flash of lightning illuminating the darkest stormy night. A simple solution to a complicated problem.

"Kiss him?"

"Yes, *liebling*. Show him how you feel through actions, not words."

"You are a treasure, my friend." She drew Gertrude close, surprising her with a warm embrace. "Thank you."

"Of course." Gertrude laughed and set her bag into her lap. Anxiety clawed at her heart as she repeatedly checked the oversized bag. It was gone. "Oh no. Where is it?" She slumped back against the chair in defeat.

"Is something the matter?"

"I cannot find my journal." She forced a nervous chuckle in an attempt to downplay the severity of the loss. "I always write down things so I remember them later when I need it." Gertrude's heart stopped. When had she lost it? She had it when she left Paris, so it must be on the train. "I can never follow my own advice, and lately I find I need all the help I can get. Perhaps I left it in my compartment."

"Well, what does it look like? I shall keep watch for it in case I see it lying on the train."

"It is a small, leather bound journal. Large enough to write comfortably, but small enough to fit in one's pocket. Or in my case, my handbag." She lifted the bag with a shrug. Damn and blast. Where could it possibly be? Perhaps the conductor found it or one of the porters, she reminded herself to ask them later.

"I shall watch for it." Matilda offered her hand.

Gertrude took it with a smile. "*Danke, liebling*." She shifted topics as to not dwell upon her own misfortunes. "And fret not, I am sure the major will come to his senses soon enough."

"I certainly hope so." Matilda seemed easily distracted by her own personal issues concerning the major. Their conversation lapsed into lighter topics.

When the lounge door opened revealing the porter, Gertrude seized her opportunity. "Excuse me. I must speak with the porter. I completely forgot to order the countess's luncheon."

"Oh, please, do not stand on ceremony for me. I shall be quite comfortable here."

She crossed the car and caught the porter's attention. "Excuse me."

"*Oui*, madame." He turned with a polite smile.

"Would you please have the countess's luncheon delivered to my room this afternoon?"

"As you wish, madame." He nodded seeming to sense her hesitation. "Is there anything else I can do for you?"

"Yes, have you seen a leather journal lying around? I seem to have misplaced mine yesterday."

"I have not seen one, madame, but I will ask the staff if they have found anything matching your description."

"*Merci.*" Gertrude resigned herself to the possibility it may be lost forever. Unless she removed it from her bag and forgot to replace it. She decided to check her compartment before allowing the panic to overwhelm her.

Suppressing her fears, she turned back to Matilda. "I must check on the countess. Do excuse me."

"Of course. I shall be here if you would like to join me again." Her young friend seemed much more relaxed with her situation. It seemed she found peace in their earlier conversation.

"Lovely." This pleased Gertrude, however her own situation, with its overlapping similarities, did not seem as complicated as she once believed.

Once she stepped from the dining car, her mind returned to the task at hand. Searching her room. As though drawn by an invisible force, Gertrude glanced up in time to see Nikolai, with his coat draped over his arm, sleeves rolled up bearing his muscular forearms. His jade eyes fixed upon her face.

She gripped the rail beside the window for support. Lord, but does he have to be so ridiculously handsome? Wearing a mask of indifference, she continued past him.

"Where are you going?" He paused beside her. The heat from his body pulsed in waves. Had he been outside working in the snow with no coat?

"To inquire if the countess requires tea." She met his gaze with bold determination. Her knees weakened at the intensity of it.

Nikolai nodded. "Will you join me for dinner this evening?"

Surprised, Gertrude studied his face searching for some indication as to his true intentions. Most times he merely dictated orders, but this request caught her unaware.

"Do I have a choice?" She gripped the rail tighter.

"Would you rather I dine with your new companion?" The corner of his lip curled in a challenging smirk.

"Very well." She straightened. "If I must."

"Until then." He tipped his head in acknowledgement and proceeded down the hall, pulling his coat on before he stepped into the dining car.

Confusion settled around her heart. What game did he play? Irritated, Gertrude continued down the corridor until she stepped into the next car. She tripped and caught herself against the wall.

She glanced down and found a leather journal lying on the floor. "There it is!" She scooped the journal up in relief and tucked it into her bag. Relief infused her.

Gertrude hugged the bag to her chest and continued down the corridor toward her compartment.

Major Montgomery burst out of his room and collided with her nearly knocking her down.

"I apologize." He rested a gentle hand on her shoulder to steady her. "Are you well?" His gaze slid over her form to ensure he had not caused harm. "Please forgive me. I...well, I have no excuse for my behavior."

"I am well." Gertrude clutched her bag tighter afraid to lose her precious journal again. "Please think nothing of it." She smiled. "Matilda is waiting for you in the dining car. I must tend to the countess."

"Yes, well, thank you for entertaining Matilda. She enjoys your company." The major tipped his head. "Have a lovely evening, Fraulein Bleul."

"You as well, Major Montgomery." Gertrude continued on to her compartment as the major set off for the dining car in the opposite direction.

Safely tucked inside her compartment, Gertrude locked the door. She pressed her hand to her throat and released a deep breath. Conflicting emotions raged inside her. What could Nikolai's purpose be in inviting her to dinner?

He never showed interest in spending time with her before. Perhaps their situation warranted a different approach to their strained working relationship. She sat at the small table and pulled the journal from her bag. After jotting down a few notes of her conversation with Matilda, she could tend to her other responsibilities.

Gertrude opened the leather cover and frowned. It was

written in English. She wrote hers in German. Scanning the pages, she recoiled in horror at the realization unfolding before her. This was not her journal, which meant one thing.

Her journal was still missing.

"No. No. No!" She shouted wanting to throw the journal to the floor. Then the polished script outlining a familiar word caught her attention.

Countess von Breunner. Nikolai. Wait? Who did this journal belong to?

She skimmed through the pages until it clicked into place. There were only two people on the train who utilized English as their first language. Matilda and Major Montgomery.

Matilda would have no use of a journal containing this type of information. This only left the major. Nikolai mentioned the major's position as the emissary to the British ambassador in Vienna. The journal must belong to him.

She scanned through the book further and noted names, locations, dates, and other information which seemed innocuous enough. The dates spanned the last few years and Nikolai's name seemed to appear quite frequently in the journal.

Then she noticed an entry in June of 1895 containing Nikolai's name. Beside it the word Okhrana and Russian secret police were scrawled in dark bold strokes. *Double agent?* Those two words lay behind them.

Gertrude's breath caught in her throat. What did this mean?

She turned to the latest entry dated just the day before.

Nikolai. Gertrude. Countess von Breunner. Five unknown passengers. Alpine Express Paris to Vienna. Suspicion of foul play. Investigate further.

Slamming the book closed, Gertrude stood quickly. She pulled down her suitcase and tossed the book inside of it before locking it. Her heart pounded.

How could she possibly face Nikolai now? He would know. What did the major mean, foul play? Questions swamped her mind in a furious onslaught.

A knock at the door made her jump.

"Who is it?"

"The porter, madam. I have the countess's luncheon."

Gertrude opened the door and accepted the tray, trying to remain calm. "*Merci.*"

The porter turned to leave.

"Wait, please." She called out in a burst of panic.

"*Oui*, madam?" He paused.

"Can you please deliver a message to my companion? He's waiting for me in the lounge."

"As you wish, madam." The porter nodded.

"Tell him I am ill and unable to join him."

The porter inclined his head without hesitation. "I will deliver the message."

"Thank you." She closed the door.

With her heart beating wildly inside her chest, Gertrude took a moment to calm her mind. Nikolai would not believe her message, but how could she possibly face him now?

She groaned and decided tonight she would join the countess for dinner, even if she was an imposter. But if the journal were correct, would that not make Nikolai a dangerous imposter as well?

At some point she had to face him, but how long could she prolong the inevitable?

CHAPTER FIVE

"A room filled with braying donkeys." Nikolai sprinkled the spice of exaggerated details onto the story. The truth was far less amusing than his own version of events. "It took hours to remove them all. The smell still lingers on damp nights."

Matilda laughed. After a short time in her company, Nikolai understood why this beautiful young woman had become such complicated burden upon Anson. She proved charming and vivacious. Her curiosity lent a sweet innocence to her personality, reaffirming his previous assertion. If Anson did not lay claim to her, someone less trustworthy would prey upon such a treasure.

His mind drifted to his own complicated entanglement. After inviting Gertrude to join him at dinner, he played the possibilities out in his mind. The journal left searing questions burning inside his mind. Ones he wished to have answered from her own lips. Some of her entries were quite passionate in their declarations.

Earlier that afternoon after the porter delivered her message, Nikolai refrained from stalking to her compartment, knocking down the door and demanding an explanation. They had just spoken, and she seemed perfectly healthy during that conversation, if not a bit uncomfortable. Perhaps he was behaving unfairly toward her since they were not exactly entirely in each other's confidences. How he wished to read her mind. What secrets did she hide in their shadowed recesses? Something made her uncomfortable to the point where she refused his company. He would draw it from her, at some point, that much was certain. He shifted in his seat and pushed the thoughts away, choosing to focus on Matilda instead.

Nikolai's attention drifted to the mirror situated on the far wall displaying a perfect reflection of door behind him leading to the lounge car. Anson's murderous expression beyond the glass nearly made him laugh. Perhaps this evening would provide a show as well as a meal and lively conversation. He sipped his wine.

Matilda moved her focus from the door and drank some wine. Her boisterous mood deflated at the appearance of the major. How delightfully dramatic.

He studied her over the crystal rim. "He is a complicated man."

"I beg your pardon." Matilda blinked twice.

"Your countenance changed. I assume my old friend finally appeared." He glanced over his shoulder even though he saw the now empty door perfectly in the reflection. "I see he chose not to join us."

"Yes, well. I believe we have reached an impasse. I do not think he desires to be in my company more than he must."

"On the contrary." Nikolai offered the insight without malicious intent. "I think he desires it more than he dare admit to anyone, especially himself."

"He knows my thoughts and feelings when it comes to our relationship, and I know his." She straightened with certainty. "He maintains I am only a child with no concept of what I desire, and he has made it perfectly clear I have no place in his life."

Matilda turned her attention to the painting on the wall. Every detail of her expression belied the inner turmoil deep in her soul. Despite her best attempts to hide it, Nikolai recognized the pain beneath her easy dismissal of Anson's rejection.

"Major Montgomery is the most honorable and patriotic man I have ever met. He has proven himself as both an ally and friend. But when it comes to matters of the heart, he is *durak*." When she blinked in confusion, he clarified. "What you would call an idiot."

Matilda smothered her laughter behind her hand and cleared her throat. "What do you mean?"

"The major has one love." Nikolai paused. "His country."

"I do not understand—"

"*Milyy rebenok.*" Nikolai laughed and shook his head. "Sweet child. He lives for his work. It has been his passion during all the time I have known him. And never have I seen him look at a woman the way he looks at you."

Matilda dropped her gaze and hid her blush behind a glass of wine. "Mr. Voronia."

"Love is nothing to be ashamed of."

"I have told him of my love."

"Words are not enough to convince a man."

"You have a point, Mr. Voronia."

Of course, he did, but when the waiter interrupted them to serve the meal, he wondered if she truly understood the implication of his cryptic words. Did it matter? Not in the slightest. Sometimes the softest touch proved to be the most effective.

Nearly halfway through their meal, Anson approached their table with Dr. Archer, the Frenchman he met the day before.

"Good evening, Dr. Archer, Mr. Montgomery. Would you care to join us?" Matilda's greeting made Anson stiffen.

Nikolai turned to face his friend and inclined his head with a smile.

"Thank you, no, Mrs. Hudson. Mr. Montgomery tells me you have injured your foot. Would you allow me to take a look at it? He voiced his concern it may need further treatment." The doctor's attention focused solely on Matilda.

"If you think it is necessary, doctor."

"Very well, shall we retreat to your compartment? I shall have the porter fetch my bag." The doctor strode off to locate the porter in the lounge car.

Matilda rose to her feet and swayed as she placed pressure on her sore foot.

Anson reached for her, but she pulled away from him. Interesting. Was it as obvious to the rest of the world as it was to Nikolai? These two were positively smitten with each other.

While the whole purpose of this journey began and proceeded for the sole purpose of uncovering the identity of the person who sent the photograph and protecting the countess's son, Nikolai enjoyed this unexpected, silent battle and playing both sides with ease.

"I am more than capable of walking unassisted, thank you." Matilda turned toward him. "I enjoyed your company and the conversation. If you will pardon me."

Bolstered into action by his antagonistic nature, Nikolai rose to his feet. "Allow me to escort you to your room. It would not be wise to over exert yourself."

The gleam of pure hatred in Anson's eyes nearly made Nikolai laugh out loud. He took Matilda's arm and helped her toward the exit. He could almost feel the jealousy radiating off Anson in waves.

He bore her weight as they walked together from the dining car. Nikolai noted the other passengers in the dining and lounge car.

The married couple sat quite content in their corner. As the doctor held the door to the lounge car, Nikolai glimpsed at the two Italian men who worked for Signora Castellan. Cigarette smoke and suspicion curled around the duo. They watched with narrowed gazes, muttering to each other as their small party passed by.

Earlier this morning, he realized why they looked so familiar. They were in the employment of Signora Castellan, the wife of the Italian ambassador. Their presence on this train needled at Nikolai's conscience. Surely, they could not have anticipated both Anson and Nikolai's presence on the train? Perhaps they had something to do with the incidents involving his compartment and Anson's. But why would they demolish one room and not the other? Something did not sit well with any of the evidence.

"Just in here." Matilda pointed to her compartment.

Nikolai helped her into her room and bowed before taking his leave to allow the doctor to examine her foot.

"Such a gentleman," Anson hissed at Nikolai under his breath.

"At least one of us behaves as such." He glanced into the room before turning back to Anson. "If you let her escape, then

I have no sympathy for the painful existence you will lead." Nikolai leaned closer and lowered his voice, playing the devil's advocate. "A very short, painful existence."

"Was that a threat?"

"Of course not, my friend." Nikolai flashed a half-hearted smile. "It was a promise. *Dobroy nochi*." He turned and strode down the corridor toward his room.

He allowed himself a small chuckle once he entered the train car containing his compartment. Never before had Anson proved this easy to antagonize. People, it seemed, were more predictable when distracted by matters of the heart. At least it left the opportunity for Nikolai to ensure his own personal details were left unscrutinized.

Unlocking his room, Nikolai paused. His gaze drifted to Gertrude's door. He inhaled deeply resigned to deal with his own inner demons.

He rapped twice on the door.

"Who is it?" Her voice sounded muted from inside.

"Nikolai." He paused for a breath. "May I come in?"

"No!" Her shout sounded much closer to the door. "I am not feeling well. Please, go."

"Gertrude." His fingers traced over the wooden frame before dropping his hand to his side. "Very well. We arrive in Salzburg in the morning. Vienna by nightfall."

"Yes, I know."

"You cannot avoid me forever, *liebling*." He smiled when no reply came. "Goodnight."

Once he found haven in his own compartment, he sat on the bed and leaned against the shared wall. Muffled noises came from inside her room. He imagined her agitated by his parting words. It gave him comfort to know he wielded such power over her, at least according to the impassioned words contained within her journal.

Nikolai pulled the worn leather journal from beneath her pillow and opened it. He skimmed through the pages until he found the small paper he left as a marker next to the entry burned into his mind.

I can no longer deny my attraction to Nikolai. Every moment I find myself in his presence, I take comfort in knowing he protects us. And yet, I allow myself the small indulgence to imagine he is there for my safety and comfort alone.

Just tonight, he stood behind me. His scent teasing me. His warmth inviting me closer. The torment is more than I can bear. Does he truly not know how much I care for him? No. And I cannot tell him.

Nikolai's heart is carved from ice. He cannot love.

With a sigh, he lay the book on his chest. If she only knew the truth, perhaps she would understand. But there was no time. Not yet. His mission lay before him. Once they reached Vienna, he would ensure her and the maid's safe return to the palace and then uncover the truth of the photograph and its sender.

She was right about one thing. He could not love, but it did not mean he had no heart.

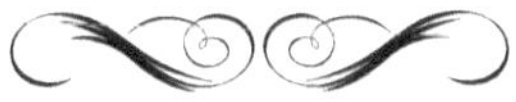

When the train pulled into Salzburg station, Gertrude had already been awake for hours. She spent the night in torment unable to sleep. Nikolai's presence seemed to permeate through the wall and wrap its ghostly fingers around her throat.

She thumbed through the journal, noting Nikolai's presence at many of the events in the major's journal, which did not seem odd considering they both moved in similar social circles thanks to their employers. The major's assertion Nikolai belonged to the Russian secret police, the Okhrana, left her disconcerted.

For years she heard the stories of the Okhrana from the countess and her children. Whispers of their deeds filtered through the household especially through anyone with ties either by employment or by blood to the Russian empire. Rumors of their deeds lay shrouded in secrecy and drenched in blood.

The more she pondered Nikolai's connection to such a group, the more concerned she became. Such an organization would be dangerous to have any connection, especially in the current political climate. The only way to be certain would be to ask him directly, but such a question would put her in an uncomfortable position. Who was Nikolai truly? For this journal confirmed the one thing she suspected for years. Nikolai Voronia was more than he seemed.

As the train slowed, a soft knock on her door broke into her harried thoughts.

"Who is it?" She leaned against the wood and listened for the reply.

"Nikolai. Open the door, *liebling*." His tone played at odds with the gentle command.

She chewed her lip afraid a confrontation with him would betray her unease.

"Open. This. Door." The command came sharp and deep, brooking no argument.

"One moment." Gertrude quickly made sure the journal lay tucked in her suitcase beneath some garments. She opened the door and braced herself for the inevitable wave of attraction that seemed to distract her in his presence.

He wore his dark blue waistcoat with the silver pattern. The color emphasized his eyes, and she leaned heavily against the door. His brow arched.

"Feeling better this morning?"

"Yes, much better. Thank you." She stepped aside and placed some of her items into the suitcase. Having something to busy her hands gave her a reprieve from his scrutiny.

"We will be arriving in Vienna by nightfall. Ensure the countess has her things prepared. I shall be taking you directly to the estate."

She glanced over her shoulder. In all the years of their acquaintance, Nikolai never explained himself. Yet this morning, he explained each step so she could be prepared. Why? The contents of the journal haunted her mind.

He stepped closer. His heat and scent coalesced around her. She fought the desire to sway back against him. "Why do you lie to me, *liebling*?"

The gentle tone of his voice nearly broke her, but she stood her ground. "Lie?" She dared to meet his gaze and licked her lips. "I never lied to you." Her hand tightened around the edge of the suitcase.

He tutted softly. "Are you sure about that?"

Gertrude wanted to slam the lid on the suitcase and run away. He was too handsome, too dangerous, too...close. She backed away from him until her thigh hit the table.

He followed, stalking steadily closer until only a breath of air lay between them. "Do I frighten you?"

"Says the wolf to a hare."

"Is that a confession?" His lips curled in humor.

"A confession of what? That you frighten me?" She laughed. "You frighten everyone, Nikolai. But not me."

"Why do you run from me if you are not frightened?" His touch burned her skin as he wrapped his fingers around her throat. "I could kill you with my bare hands before you could scream."

She trembled beneath the touch. Her mind raged against the evil thoughts conjured by the journal's words. "If you wanted me dead, you would have done so already."

His eyes darkened before he released her and stepped away. "Finish packing. I will fetch you when we reach Vienna." He walked out of her room and closed the door behind him.

Gertrude collapsed against the window and pressed a hand to her racing heart. Her fingertips traced the place Nikolai's touch branded her. Was he jesting? Why did it feel much more intimate than a teasing threat?

Another knock at the door startled her.

"Who is it?"

"Matilda."

Attempting to steel her nerves, she opened the door.

"*Guten Morgen.*" Matilda's effervescence warmed her.

"*Guten Morgen, liebling.*" Gertrude invited Matilda into her compartment. "Please come in. I trust you slept well."

"I slept so well, I nearly missed Salzburg completely."

Gertrude pushed thoughts of Nikolai aside and focused on Matilda's excitement. "We will only be here for a short while. By nightfall we shall be in Vienna."

"I wish I could have seen the city. I hear Salzburg is

beautiful."

"It is." Gertrude opened the curtains, revealing the platform and the station beyond. "Perhaps one day you can return and enjoy the delights this region has to offer."

"Perhaps." Matilda distracted herself with the view of the platform outside.

Gertrude lingered behind her still attempting to calm her heart after her conversation with Nikolai. She recognized the major as he crossed the platform. He certainly was a handsome man.

"I see the major decided to stretch his legs a bit." Gertrude grinned.

"Mmmhmm." Matilda's distracted reply made her shake her head. If only she could explain to this sweet girl how complicated love truly made things. But Matilda had eyes for the major alone, and Gertrude knew nothing she said would change her mind. Besides, had she not offered advice on how to capture the major's attention?

The conductors whistle echoed outside. They would be leaving Salzburg in a few moments.

"*Liebling*, have you come to an understanding with the handsome major? Or is he still adamant in his refusal?"

The train whistle blared twice before falling silent, and the train lurched into motion. Both she and Matilda swayed, bracing their hands on the wall. Once they found their footing, the younger woman turned to face her.

"I believe we have. I took your and Mr. Voronia's advice."

Gertrude nearly fell over at the statement. "Nikolai gave you advice?"

"Well, yes, in a way."

"What did he suggest?" Gertrude could not imagine Nikolai offering any type of advice that could prove helpful in such a situation.

"He suggested I tell Anson of my love. I told him I did as much and been rebuffed, thrice. Then he observed sometimes actions are much better than words."

"*Och, mein Gott in Himmel.*" Gertrude sat on her bed and

pressed her hand to her mouth. What could have possessed him to say such a thing? Was he mad? But had she not offered a similar piece of advice herself? Perhaps they were both mad. He was not wrong, but how could he be so blind?

Gertrude dropped her hand and choked laughter bubbled from the depths of her soul. "Nikolai knows nothing of a woman's heart."

"Well, you did tell me to kiss him first. Is this not similar in a way?"

"I suppose that is true," Gertrude agreed. "So, you took my advice?"

"Yes." Matilda touched her lips and her eyes glazed as though transported to another plain of existence.

"I have half a mind to follow your lead." Jealousy gripped her. Perhaps she should take her own advice, and yet there were far too many questions unanswered for her to even contemplate kissing Nikolai without demanding the truth.

"Perhaps you should."

"I have no intention of being bound to any man, and Nikolai Voronia is full of dark secrets and sweet lies." Gertrude tensed letting her gaze linger on the passing scenery. When she met Matilda's gaze, she brightened. The poor girl must think her truly mad now.

A great pounding commenced on the wall behind Gertrude.

"What was that?" Matilda jumped.

"Oh, the countess. I should fetch her breakfast." She opened the suitcase on the bed and removed an apron. What on earth could she want now?

"I have not seen her during the trip. Does she not feel well?"

"The countess dislikes traveling, although she does it quite frequently. I believe it is the novelty of changing cities which fortifies her for the trip itself." Gertrude tied on the apron making a show of her duty to the imposter countess. "She dislikes eating in public, so I bring meals to her compartment."

"Would you like some help?"

Another series of blows shook the wall. Matilda's eyes

widened. Something was wrong.

"No, thank you. I must go. Shall we meet for afternoon tea?"

"That sounds lovely."

"I shall see you then." Without another thought, Gertrude hurried from the room and knocked on the door.

"Who is it?" the maid hissed.

"Who do you think?" The door swung open and Gertrude slipped inside. "What is all this commotion?"

The maid wore one of the countess's old gowns in preparation for their arrival in Vienna. She thrust a paper at Gertrude, her eyes wide with fear.

"What is it?"

"A note. Someone slipped it beneath the door for the countess."

Gertrude unfolded the paper.

Your guard dog is useless. Send him home. You shall find further instructions upon your return. Tell no one or he dies.

Gertrude gasped. "You just received this?"

The maid nodded.

"Have you told Nikolai?"

"No. I just received it, miss."

She folded the note and put it in her pocket. "I will relay this to him telling him I intercepted it. Say nothing of it to anyone. I do not want you involved in whatever this is."

"Of course." The maid fidgeted with the hem of the expensive gown.

"Now, sit down, I will fix your hair." Gertrude took the brush and combed through the maid's dark tresses. As she worked, her mind turned over and over the meaning of the note. Who could have sent it? What did they mean? Did it have something to do with the photograph the countess received in Paris? Or was this an attack on Nikolai from someone on the train?

Whatever it led to, Gertrude knew she had to tell Nikolai, but this was neither the time nor the place. First, she had to retrieve the letter waiting at the countess's estate, then she would confront Nikolai.

Chapter Six

Walking away from Gertrude proved more difficult than Nikolai ever imagined. Having her so close, feeling her pulse beneath his fingertips while her scent filled his thoughts with delightful temptation, nearly broke his reserve. He knew her secrets, gleaned them from the pages of her journal, an insight he could thoroughly exploit, and yet he refrained. Not for lack of desire, no. There were pressing issues to address before he could lay his claim to her.

He stepped into his room as Matilda appeared at the end of the corridor. He closed the door softly.

He waited a few moments allowing his heated blood to cool. Gertrude unraveled him like no other woman. He wished the mystery of the photograph and its threatening note were solved already.

The muted voices of the two women echoed through the wall. Nikolai glimpsed at himself in the small mirror beside the door. He straightened his jacket and smoothed his hair looking far more confident than he felt. The conductor's whistle sounded from the platform outside the window.

Only a few hours remained until they reached Vienna, then he could solve this damned mystery and be done with it.

Quietly, he exited his room locking the door behind him and venturing down the corridor. When he reached the sleeper car before the lounge, he spied Anson at the other end having just reboarded the train.

"Good morning, my friend. Care to join me?" Nikolai needed a distraction.

Anson shuffled in agitation. "I must check on Matilda."

He rested his hand on Anson's shoulder. "She is in Gertrude's compartment."

"Perhaps I should check—"

"She is safe. Believe me." Nikolai smirked and clapped his hand on his back. "You can tell me all about your conquest while we break our fast."

Anson followed him toward the dining car.

"What happened last evening?"

"A gentleman would never ask such a question." Anson shifted his attention to the window as the train lurched into motion.

"I have never claimed to be a gentleman, major, and you know this. We have shared many tales. I remember you once told me about a lewd show you attended in Istanbul. What are a few intimate details among friends?" Why it delighted him to dig his talons into the major's sensitive wound, he could not comprehend, and yet he craved a distraction from his own painful desires.

"Nothing happened." Anson's jaw twitched with irritation as he turned to face him.

"Nothing?" Disappointment filled him. He hoped his well-placed suggestion during dinner the evening before would spur the young woman into action. "Not even a kiss."

Anson groaned, and his gaze glossed over as he surrendered to whatever thoughts came to mind.

Nikolai grinned. "She took my advice then."

"Advice?" Anson snapped and leaned across the table. "What the hell are you talking about? What did you tell her to do?"

"Nothing as vulgar as you would believe. I merely advised to take the first step, since you seemed so adamant to play the gentleman."

"How could you do such a thing? She is only a child." Rage appeared to consume Anson as his face turned a violent shade of red.

Nikolai's humor dissolved instantly. "She is no child, Anson. In case you have not yet realized it, she loves you." He folded his arms across his chest. Jealousy pierced his soul. "You are a fool if you cannot realize what a valuable treasure you have before you waiting to be claimed."

"I have nothing to offer her. No title, no land, no wealth, no security. I can never return to England. She deserves someone in their prime with the world at his feet." Anson avoided his gaze once more.

"If you truly believe such rubbish, then I pity you. You will regret this." Nikolai jabbed his index finger against the table with emphasis wanting to expand upon his assertion, but unable to tear down the invisible barrier he built around himself over the years. "Believe me."

"At this moment, the only thing I regret is not turning you into the Royal guards when I had the chance." The vehemence in Anson's words stung.

"Do not threaten me." He lowered his tone, every syllable laced with menace. "We both share equal blame for that night."

"And I paid my penance for it." Anson stood and glared down at him. "You hid. Coward." He turned and stormed from the dining car.

Nikolai pulled the flask from his pocket and unscrewed the top. He took a long drought and hissed as the liquor burned straight to his gut.

After all those years of tenuous friendship, it finally snapped. Perhaps he pressed too hard, teasing Anson about his newfound paramour. Had it not been for his determination to distract Anson from the truth of his journey back to Vienna, he would not have pried so heavily into his friend's personal life.

His gaze fixed on the mountains outside the window. Since when had he become so heavy handed? Nikolai beat down the regret clawing at him. Once they returned to Vienna and he had answers, then he would set right his friendship with Anson. And yet, those parting words burned into his gut, staining his soul with guilt.

He was right. They both shouldered the blame for the events of the night so long ago, and Anson paid a high price for the outcome. Nikolai could not bear to tell him he too paid a high price for his role in those events.

Stuffing his flask in his pocket, Nikolai retreated to his room and packed his suitcase. Soon they would arrive in Vienna, and there would be no time to waste.

When the train came to a stop at Vienna station, Nikolai ensured both the countess and Gertrude were ready to depart. He hired a carriage to carry them directly to the countess's estate.

No one questioned the countess's quick pace or the fact she wore her heavy winter furs which concealed part of her face. Nikolai spotted Anson and Matilda on the station platform but ignored the guilt twisting in his gut. No. He would fix it later. He must complete the mission first.

The decoy countess and Gertrude rode inside the carriage while Nikolai sat with the driver. It took strength of will to stop himself from pulling Gertrude into his embrace when she placed her hand in his to enter the carriage.

He steeled himself against the evening chill, bundling deeper inside his woolen great coat and tipping his hat down tighter on his head.

Once they reached the estate, he led the ladies to the door. The maid pretending to be the countess disappeared inside the warm interior, but Gertrude drew up short and turned to face him.

"I must speak with you." Her gaze shifted suspiciously from left to right.

"It must wait." Nikolai refused to waver no matter how much he longed to take her in his arms and hear her confession. "Where is the butler?"

Gertrude's expression fell. She grasped his arm. "No. Now."

The butler appeared in the doorway. "Is there something you need, Mr. Voronia?"

"Have I received any correspondence?"

"No, sir."

"I see." He shook his head. Perhaps something had been delivered to his apartment.

Gertrude stood before him, her jaw set.

"Stay here. I shall return post haste." He turned and retreated down the path.

"Nikolai, come back!" Gertrude called after him.

He ignored her, choosing to focus on the task at hand and ignore the pleas of his heart to return to her side.

The walk to his apartment from the estate took fifteen minutes. He climbed the five flights of stairs and unlocked the door to his small sanctuary. Inside, he found a small pile of mail on the floor.

He gathered the letters and sorted through them. Nothing of possible connection to the photograph and the note lay within its contents.

"Damn it." He tossed the letters aside and poured himself a drink. Tossing it back, he welcomed the bite of the vodka.

He paced the length of the room, his gaze settling on the hallway door. Perhaps the letter had been delivered to the estate. He needed to check there before considering any other possibilities.

Slowly he rechecked the pile of letters, thumbing through them one at a time. Still, he found nothing of any consequence.

Nikolai leaned against the mantle and took a deep breath replaying the contents of the original message on the back of the photograph in Paris.

The knock on the door brought him up short, and he reached for the pistol tucked into his waistband. No one but the countess and Anson knew where he kept his apartment, and the countess was still in Paris.

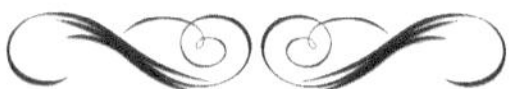

Nikolai left her no alternative. She straightened to her full height and knocked on the door. When it swung open under her hand, she shrieked when her gaze fixed on the barrel of the gun pointed directly at her head.

"What in the devil are you doing here?" Nikolai scowled and dropped the pistol to his side before snatching her by the wrist and dragging her into his apartment.

She spun around as he released her. He glanced into the hallway and then locked the door.

When he turned to face her, a murderous glint in the depth of his gaze betrayed his displeasure. "Did you follow me?"

"Tonight?" she hedged trying to calm the racing of her heart. Her gaze flickered to the pistol in his grip.

He inclined his head as to imply *of course* in an exasperated manner.

"Not tonight, no." She squared her shoulders.

His brow arched. "You followed me before?"

"Accidentally." Gertrude sniffed. "I saw you one day in the market. I followed for a while and found this place. I assumed it was your personal apartment the countess mentioned."

He uncocked the pistol and tucked it into the back of his waistband. Gertrude could not tell if he was angry with her or impressed. He merely nodded in his stoic manner.

She smoothed her hand over the front of her wool cloak.

"Why are you here?" His tone mimicked a growl.

"To give you this." She thrust the note they received on the train as well as a letter she found in the pile of mail after he left the countess's estate. It was the same sloppy handwriting.

He snatched the letters from her hand and ripped them open.

"I tried to tell you about them earlier, but you refused to listen." Gertrude shrugged her shoulder in a careless manner. Her insides fluttered with agitation. Nothing good would come of either of these letters, she could tell.

A dark cloud settled over Nikolai's expression as he read. His stormy gaze locked with hers. "Have you read these?"

"Only the first one, I...intercepted it on the train. The porter delivered it to the countess." His agitation soured into something much more vile. Gertrude took a step back.

"And this one?" He lifted the paper in his right hand.

Gertrude shook her head. "I found it in the countess's letters when we returned to the estate. I took it when I recognized the handwriting."

"You've shown no one else?"

"I showed no one but you." Gertrude braced her hand on the table beside her and licked her lips. She wished herself anywhere but there. His expression shifted into something otherworldly, something dangerous. It terrified her as much as it excited her. She pushed the conundrum aside. "Why? Is the countess in danger?"

"No." Nikolai shook his head and took a deep breath. "I cannot allow you to return to the estate."

The flutter transformed into full-fledged panic. She rounded the small table as he stalked closer. "What do you mean I cannot return? I must return. The countess..."

"The countess knows you are safe, and that is all she needs to know." He rounded the table coming closer.

Gertrude darted toward the door and grasped the handle. Before she could unlock it, his hand slammed down against the wooden paneling. She shrieked and spun around. His gaze bore into hers.

"You involved yourself in this, *liebling*. Now, you will play it out to its conclusion." Nikolai pushed away from her with a smirk.

She fumbled with the lock and pulled the door open. Before she made it to the first step, he snatched her by the waist.

"Let me go! Put me down!" She swore at him in German as he picked her up and laid her over his shoulder. With both fists she beat on him, flailing her feet until he smacked her bottom with his open palm.

"Do not make me put you over my knee, *liebling*." His voice sent a shiver of need and fear intertwined through her heart.

He quickly locked the door and descended the stairs. Gertrude glanced up to see an old man standing on the landing above her shaking his head, his lips pressed into a thin line of distaste.

"Help me!" she called.

Nikolai swatted her backside once more. "Do not make me tell you again." He descended five flights of stairs with her sitting like a sack of flour over his shoulder.

When they reached the ground floor, he set her on her feet and grasped her wrist, pulling her close.

She gasped.

"Where I go, you go. There is no discussion. Behave, or I shall punish you. The countess's life is at stake, do you understand?"

Gertrude stilled at his words and swallowed the lump in her throat. She nodded weakly. "I understand."

"Good." He stood to his full height, towering above her. "Now. We will be returning to the train station. Do not ask questions. Do not argue. Follow my instruction. Is that clear?"

Gertrude could do nothing but nod. Her heart twisted in knots. What would become of the countess? What would become of her? Even though fear coursed through her veins, at some elemental level, Gertrude trusted Nikolai. After all, he swore to protect the countess and her family. *But you are not family.* Her mind whispered. *He does not love you.*

Before she could dwell on the thoughts raining down upon her, Nikolai took her hand and led her from his apartment. He hailed a cab and within minutes they were deposited at the steps of the Vienna train station.

He helped her from the carriage and interlaced their fingers. Heat spread through her at the intimate contact. Even through the fabric of the gloves, the warmth of his touch burned her. To anyone passing by, they would see a couple madly in love, but Gertrude knew the slightest betrayal of this image would cause more harm to her situation. Nikolai was not a man to be crossed.

The well-lit station seemed quite deserted. Nikolai bought two tickets for the ten o'clock train returning east stopping in Salzburg and Munich before returning to Paris.

"Are we returning to Paris?" Gertrude asked as they walked onto the platform.

"No." Nikolai checked his watch. "The train departs in ten minutes. Should anyone ask, we are married and are returning to visit family in Salzburg."

Gertrude's head ached even as her heart leapt at the idea of being married to Nikolai, even if it were only an act. Try to hate him though she might, he would not let harm come to her. That knowledge left her with a sliver of trust which she relinquished even as her mind raged against it.

"Do not leave my side, do you understand?" His tone commanded compliance.

"Yes." She tried to pull her hand from his, but he tightened his grip. "Must you be so forceful?"

"Must you be so obstinate?"

"I have agreed to your demands and I will follow your instructions, but I deserve to know what I am involved in." She scowled. "I have been..."

"Shh." His gloved fingertip touched her lips, but his attention shifted to the platform around them like a predator sensing the arrival of prey. He tugged on her hand as he closed the gap to the train.

Once they boarded, Nikolai located their compartment and sealed them inside being sure to draw the shades across the windows.

Gertrude sat near the window and rest her head against the wall. What madness did she find herself tangled in?

Nikolai sat across from her and pulled the two letters from his pocket. Quietly he studied them.

When the train whistle sounded and the lumbering engine departed the station, the tension between them tore her sanity in two.

"I have been patient for far too long, Nikolai." She crossed her arms. "I demand to know the meaning of those letters. Do they have something to do with the photograph the countess received in Paris?" Her frown deepened when he did not reply. "Nikolai Voronia, answer me, *Verdammt*." She swung her foot at his leg.

He caught her ankle in his hand. How did he move so quickly? His gaze slid up from the letters. The intensity left her breathless and trembling. The pressure of his fingertips against her stocking clad ankle sent a shiver of awareness through her. He stroked his thumb along the seam of her stocking, up and down beneath the hem of her skirt.

Every fiber of her being railed against his intrusive behavior, and yet she had longed for his attention for so long this single touch left her desperate for more. He dropped her foot to the floor with a thud.

Bereft at the loss, she glared harder. "I despise you."

He cocked his head and studied her. "I doubt it."

She threw her bag at him. It collided with his shoulder and the contents spilled onto the floor between them. The journal landed on top of his foot.

Before she could stop him, he picked it up. "What is this?" He opened it and scanned the contents. His curiosity faded as he flipped through the pages. When he met her gaze, his lips thinned. A muscle in his jaw pulsed.

She had seen him upset before, but it did not compare to being on the receiving end of this murderous glare.

"Where did you get this?" He shook the journal.

"I found it. On the Alpine Express." She swallowed the fear congealing in her throat stealing her voice. "I misplaced my journal, so when I found this one, I assumed it was mine. When I realized the mistake..." She chewed on her lip as shame overwhelmed her. "I should have returned it. But I did not."

"Why?"

"I do not know." She twisted her apron between her fingers. "Because of what it says. The major watches everything."

"I know." He leaned forward, pressing into her space. "What does it say?"

With a glance to heaven, she inhaled deep. "He knows you are Okhrana. He does not trust you."

"Of course, he does not trust me." Nikolai leaned back and lounged against the seat with ease. "But it is not his opinion which matters to me, *liebling*."

Gertrude shivered at the calculating gleam in his eyes and the smirk playing on his lips. Handsome as the devil and twice as sinful, this man with his countless secrets, had drawn her into his den. But to what end?

CHAPTER SEVEN

While he relished the idea of being alone with Gertrude, this was not at all how he had envisioned it. Finding her on his doorstep filled him with mixed emotions. This was not the time or the place for a romantic interlude. Her revelations merely fueled the already conflicting halves of his mind.

He glanced down at the letters in one hand and the journal in the other. The treasure trove of information contained within this leather-bound book piqued his interest. But he found himself more interested in exactly how and when it came into the possession of the woman sitting across from him.

Nikolai tucked the letters into the journal and set it aside. "Get comfortable. It will be several hours until we reach Salzburg."

Gertrude unclasped the cloak and pulled it off her shoulders. "Always so demanding. Are you incapable of asking in a polite manner? Or does it delight you to issue orders?" She folded her arms across her chest, emphasizing her bosom beneath the fabric.

God, help him. This woman challenged him daily for the last five years, if she continued to push him, he would show her how commanding he could be.

He forced a tone of civility. "Perhaps we should begin again."

"Today? This week?" She cocked her head. Those cornflower blue eyes brimmed with distrust. "Or shall we go back to the beginning?"

The night she referred to appeared fresh and vivid in his mind as it had for every day over the duration of their acquaintance. He admired her spirit and beauty, and his appreciation for both had not lost its potency. However, the sharp edge of her tongue left him with more scars than he cared to count. Even he knew a kitten bared her claws when threatened...or after severe neglect or abuse. He often saw how the ravages of such struggles left a heart hardened. Not unlike his own.

"Which do you prefer?" He studied her carefully.

The graceful arch of her brow rose in surprise. Skepticism quickly replaced it. "I would prefer if you would tell me the truth."

"Have I ever lied to you, *liebling*?"

"Honestly, I have no idea. I do not even attempt to understand you, Nikolai. No one knows anything of your past. You never talk about yourself." Her lips thinned.

"What do you wish to know?" Had he not found her journal, known the innermost desires of her heart, he would never have allowed himself to ask such a question. His mission was to protect those in his care, and part of that entailed keeping his own thoughts and past under lock and key.

Truth was, he wanted her to trust him implicitly. The only way to earn trust was to offer his own in return. Carefully, he searched for a way to entice her.

A crease formed between her brows. "How do I know you will not lie to me?"

"On my mother's grave." He leaned closer and held her gaze steady. "I swear to tell you nothing but the truth."

Gertrude licked her lips. "Very well."

He settled against the cushion and draped his arm across the back of the seat. "What do you wish to know?"

"Is Nikolai Voronia your real name?" Her eyes flashed with heat and curiosity.

"Yes."

"Were you in the military when you met Major Montgomery?"

"Yes."

"How did you meet him?"

Tension pulled tight across his shoulders. He never recounted that night to anyone aloud before. The events played over and over in his mind, and yet he never allowed himself to speak of it. He inhaled deeply.

"I worked as a guard at the Winter Palace. The major and his party arrived one afternoon and I was tasked as their escort during their stay at the palace." He paused searching for the simplest way to explain the events which transpired. "The major and his men found themselves in an unfortunate situation one evening with a local group of ruffians. I stepped in and saved the major's life."

Gertrude's soft lips parted in a gasp.

He steered his attention away from the temptation. "Unfortunately, the duke, whom the major protected, was killed in retaliation. I hold some of the blame for this since it was my resistance in reporting the incident to my superiors which led to the duke's death."

"What happened?"

"I tried to intercede on the major's behalf, but they would not listen. The Russian monarchy wanted nothing to do with the bloody affair. The major was tried for his negligence which led to the duke's death and banned from returning to England for the remainder of his life."

A grunt of indignation brought his attention back to Gertrude. "Why did you not come to the major's aid?"

"I could say pride, but the truth is quite simple." He shrugged. "The major denied my involvement."

"Why would he do that?"

"I do not know." The story poured from him with little effort. He shifted in his seat. "Any other questions you wish to pose?"

"Are you Okhrana?"

"I was. For several years until I met the countess and she asked me to become her personal guard." A lopsided smile curved his lips. "You wish to know how I met the countess?"

A hint of crimson stained her cheeks, but she met his gaze boldly. "Yes."

"I saved her son from being killed by a group of men he tried to cheat while playing cards." Nikolai shrugged. "It is rather anticlimactic. The countess's son, no more than nineteen, decided to try his hand at one of the more dangerous gambling dens in Moscow. As a reward for saving her son, she offered me a permanent position in her house as her personal guard."

"Why?" Gertrude asked seemingly unconvinced by the story. "What would make her ask you to become her personal guard after one encounter?"

Nikolai paused. He never questioned it before, merely took it as an omen of good fortune and grasped it with both hands. "Why question fate?"

Gertrude's laughter filled the small space. "You, the man who questions everything, chose this life because fate led you to it?"

"I did not always question everything." He scowled unnerved by her humor. "Perhaps I should have. It would have saved me much heartache and disappointment."

"Do you still believe in fate?"

"Of course." He cocked his head. "What about you, *liebling?* Do you believe in fate?"

Gertrude shook her head. "No. I do not believe in fate. I chose my path, and I will follow it to the end." The resolution in her tone took him by surprise. A story lay beneath her vehement declaration. He wondered how best to draw it from her perfect lips.

"Let me ask you a question now." He leaned forward, resting his elbows on his knees and meeting her gaze.

She drew back, eyes wide. "What could you possibly want to know about me?"

"Everything, *liebling.* Everything." He grinned.

"You get one question."

"How unfair. I answered your questions with honesty and all I get in return in one question?" He pouted, mimicking her own expression.

"One. Question." Her jaw set with finality. Fire sparked in her eyes.

Nikolai tamed the beast raging within him. He could see through the façade to the root of her desire. The journal told him what his heart already knew. She desired him, and he would have the truth from her before playing his hand. He enjoyed the game far too much to concede this quickly.

"Very well." He cleared his throat. "Did you steal the major's journal?"

Gertrude leapt to her feet. "I am not a thief! I found the journal in the corridor of the train." She paced the small space and turned on him in a fury. "I wanted to return it, but I could not bring myself to do so once I saw..." She sat down on the far end of the car. "Your name."

"Ah, you were trying to protect me?" His heart softened at her declaration.

"No." She glared. "Why would you of all people need protecting?"

"Why would you of all people try to protect me?"

She harrumphed and crossed her arms turning to face the opposite direction. "I should have told the major you stole the damned thing."

"Gertrude..."

"I am done talking to you." She turned her back to him and ceased conversation.

Nikolai wanted more from her, but it would take time to draw her into his confidence. And considering the contents of the note, time would be in abundance once they reached the countess's hunting lodge. The letter told him to wait there for further instructions.

Whoever sent this wished to ensure their own swift demise, of this Nikolai was certain. The hunted had now become the hunter.

While the journey from Vienna to Salzburg proved uneventful, it provided Gertrude with ample time to accept the situation in which she found herself. Nikolai offered no further information to clarify the contents of the letters or the reason for their immediate departure from Vienna.

Several times she opened her mouth determined to demand an explanation. But she refused to engage in another conversation with him. His sudden revelations and the blatant honesty in response to her questions of his past left her quite shaken. She wanted to know more about him, did she not? And yet, peeling back the layers to this complicated man left her feeling as though they had engaged in something intimate and forbidden. Dare she allow herself to fall deeper into a sea of conflicting emotions regarding him when she was already drowning?

By mid-morning, they were bundled together in a carriage climbing higher into the hills surrounding Salzburg. Gertrude did not recognize the area. Weaving through the mountain passes, they stumbled into a forest tucked between the mountains.

"Where are we going?" Gertrude's teeth chattered from the cold. It sank through the layers of blankets and wool garments.

"Count Von Breunner's hunting lodge." Nikolai steered the shaggy horse deeper into the woods. A thin blanket of snow dusted the ground covering the overgrown road.

"Hunting lodge?" Gertrude searched through the trees for any sign of life. "It does not look like anyone has been here in a long time."

"The countess rarely comes here. The count and his sons have not used the lodge in many years." He remained focused on the road ahead.

"But you have been here?"

"Several times."

The snow-covered ground muffled the horses' progress through the forest. A flutter of unease settled in the pit of Gertrude's stomach. After much of her time spent in Vienna, Paris, Munich, and countless other cities over the last five years, the peaceful stillness of the forest seemed eerie and disjointed from reality. She shifted on the bench beside Nikolai.

"Are you cold?" His voice sent a shiver through her.

"Yes." She burrowed deeper into the blanket.

"We will arrive soon."

The sway of the carriage pushed them together. Her gaze

lingered on the leather reins laced through his fingers.

Gertrude pushed aside the awkwardness of the silence and focused instead on the beauty of the trees and the mountains surrounding them. The scenery tugged at her memories unraveling the ones she buried so long ago. Her parents farm tucked in a row of trees at the base of the mountains. Her siblings' laughter echoing across the fields in summer. Until one day it vanished in a plume of smoke. She shook the memory from her thoughts.

Nikolai wrapped his arm around her shoulder and drew her close to his side. She stiffened at the action, unsure of how to react. He radiated heat and it slowly permeated the wool of her cloak sinking into her chilled bones. She leaned her weight against him and sighed at the flood of warmth.

Ahead in the distance, the shadows dispersed through the trees revealing a small clearing. In the middle of the clearing were several buildings. The sloped roofs and wooden shutters resembled the cottages in the town where she was raised. A tendril of smoke curled up from the chimney.

The carriage came to a stop beyond the first building. "Go inside. I will tend to the horse."

Gertrude climbed down from the carriage and approached the cottage desperate for warmth and food. Her stomach growled in protest. The small meal they had at the station that morning did nothing to sate her hunger.

She knocked on the door before opening it. "Hello." She peered inside. A fire burned in the hearth in the main room. Several chairs and a table sat by the window. Two oversized chairs stand sentinel on either side of the hearth. No one greeted her.

Stepping inside, she glanced around searching for signs of life and latched the door behind her. "Hello. Is anyone there?"

No response came. Gertrude crossed the room to the hearth and sat in the seat nearest to the fire. Her body relaxed as the warmth returned to her fingers and toes. She sank deeper into the chair and sighed.

The door swung open with a bang. A figure stepped

through the doorway.

Gertrude shot to her feet clutching her cloak tightly, her gaze drifting to the iron poker next to the fire. Her heart raced until the figure turned to face her.

Nikolai closed the door behind him and dusted his hands off on his trousers. He glanced around the room. "Where is the groundskeeper?"

She spun around. "There was no one here when I entered."

"Perhaps he is out hunting." Nikolai gestured to the fire. "Sit down. Warm yourself."

Gertrude resumed her seat choosing to keep her cloak wrapped tightly around her. "Where are you going?"

"I must speak with the groundskeeper." He pinned her with a pointed glance. "Do not venture out alone, do you understand?"

She nodded and he once again disappeared out into the cold. The sun dropped behind the mountains. It would be dark soon. Gertrude wondered if she should search for something to make for supper.

Fully revived by the warmth of the fire, she shed her cloak and wandered into the small kitchen area. A pantry lay stocked with cured meats, bread, jars of vegetables, dried herbs, and containers full of supplies designed to last the winter months.

It had been a long time since she prepared a meal for herself, let alone anyone else. The haunting memories rushed in to fill her mind. The last time had been for her husband. She blinked away the intrusive thoughts. *No. I will not waste another moment's thought on him.*

The door burst open and two men entered the cottage this time. Gertrude backed against the wall in a poor attempt to hide herself. Her heart stopped between beats.

"Gertrude." Nikolai's voice cut across the room.

With a sigh, she stepped out into the light. "I am here."

The second man closed the door. He wore a hunters cap. A grey beard covered half his face. He stepped closer and placed two rabbits upon the table. "Good day, ma'am. Sorry to give you a fright."

"Quite all right." Gertrude returned his kind smile. She admired the sparkle in his dark eyes.

"Just give me a moment and I shall get a stew on the fire." He pulled his coat off and hung it on the wall.

"Is there anything I can do to help?" she offered ignoring Nikolai's intrusive gaze.

"If you chop those vegetables there, I can skin these hares right quick. We shall have a fine meal in no time." The man turned to Nikolai. "Would you fetch some water?"

Nikolai's jaw twitched as he picked up the pail, but he nodded and retreated out into the cold once more.

"What be your name, ma'am?" The groundskeeper sat at the table and pulled a knife from his belt.

"Gertrude." She gathered some vegetables and set to cutting them.

"Ah, a lovely name for a lovely lady." The older man chuckled. "I am Lorenzo, groundskeeper for Masthead Lodge for nigh on thirty years."

"You have lived here for thirty years?" Gertrude asked.

"No, I have lived here my whole life. I have only been groundskeeper for the last thirty years." He laughed. Using his knife, he deftly skinned both hares in no time at all.

Nikolai returned with the pail of water and set it on the table where they worked.

"It must get lonely here." Gertrude studied the man's profile as he worked, pointedly ignoring Nikolai's presence.

"It does, especially these last two years. My wife passed three winters ago. God rest her soul." He crossed himself.

"Oh, I apologize. My condolences." Gertrude bit her lip and focused on the task before her.

"God takes us in his time." Lorenzo offered sagely. He rose and placed a large pot over the fire. "Place those vegetables in this pot. These two will make a fine stew."

Gertrude added the vegetables after he poured the water into the pot over the fire. Then he tossed the rabbits whole into the pot. He stirred in some herbs and nodded with a grin.

The scent of rabbit stew slowly filled the room. Gertrude's

mouth watered.

"Well then, you can use the room upstairs. I will take the room down here." Lorenzo pointed to the back wall where a door stood in the corner. "I am sure you will find it to your liking."

Nikolai appeared at her side and hooked his arm through hers. "Come with me."

She jumped at his touch but followed his lead. He gestured for her to ascend the narrow staircase first. She obliged but the awareness of his proximity burned like the hottest flame. At the top of the stairs, she opened a door which led to a spacious room.

No fire burned in the hearth. She shivered at the chill lingering in the space. It seemed clean enough. A wardrobe stood against one wall, opposite lay a window, and in the center of the room sat an oversized bed.

Gertrude spun to face Nikolai. "You cannot be serious." Panic seized her. "I will not share a bed with you."

Nikolai ignored her, kneeling by the hearth to build a fire. As he worked, she rounded on him.

"What game are you at? Does he believe we are married?" Pleasure at the thought of them being married overwhelmed the immediate horror.

"I told him nothing." Nikolai struck a match and held it to the tinder.

"Why did you not correct him?" She propped her hands on her hips.

"What good will that serve? Will it protect your modesty? Defend your innocence?" Nikolai glanced up from the smoldering fire.

Anger coiled tight in her chest. While his claims made a valid point, it did nothing to quell the unease spreading through her. Unease seemed to be the root of it all.

"Are you worried I will steal your innocence, *liebling*?" He rose to his feet and closed the space between them.

"No." She licked her lips and faced him in defiance. "I have no innocence to steal."

Nikolai tilted his head and studied her for a moment before brushing his fingertip along her jaw. Her eyes drifted closed at the touch. "I doubt that, *liebling*. I doubt it very much."

He dropped his hand and turned to leave. In the doorway, he paused. "I have told you before. You have nothing to fear from me."

Gertrude collapsed onto the bed. Her heart pounding and her mind racing. He may not know it, but she had everything to fear when it came to Nikolai. If only he knew the truth.

CHAPTER EIGHT

Too many questions remained unanswered. Nikolai returned downstairs leaving Gertrude to take some time alone. Truth was, it physically pained him to be in her presence. Thankfully he mastered his restraint long ago. But if one thing could sway him into breaking it, it would be her.

Lorenzo glanced up when he entered the room. "Such a lovely wife you have." He winked. "You are a lucky man, my friend."

Nikolai did not have the heart to correct him. Not that it mattered. Once he met with whomever sent the letter, they could return to Vienna.

The letter. The contents played over and over in his mind. *Masthead Lodge. Come alone or those you love will pay dearly for your treason.* And the note Gertrude received on the train. *Your guard dog is useless. Send him home. You shall find further instructions upon your return. Tell no one or he dies.*

The directions were meant for the countess, this much was evident. But the lack of specifics left a thread of unease unraveling in the pit of his stomach. Dare he tug on it and see where it led? Why give such vague instructions? The countess assumed her son was the potential target of this unknown villain's wrath, but it never mentioned his name specifically. Perhaps they meant the count or another of her household. Still, the mystery puzzled him.

He collapsed on the chair by the fire sprawling his legs out. "Has anyone been to the lodge?"

Lorenzo stirred the stew in the large cast iron pot. "Aside from myself, no. The count has not returned to hunt in many years. Although I still receive the funds to maintain the property, it sits in disuse." He tisked. "Quite a shame really. A lovely place in the mountains should not sit empty. Damn shame."

"A shame indeed." Nikolai's stomach growled at the savory aroma drifting up from the stewpot over the fire. "Has anyone from the village come around?"

"In the summers I hire a few of the young lads to help keep the grounds and fix things around the house." Lorenzo furrowed his brow in thought and then shook his head. "No one since fall harvest."

The demand to meet here certainly made sense. Isolated, damn near deserted, which provided the perfect setting to ambush and kill an unskilled target. If they expected the countess to come alone, then they most certainly meant her harm. He needed to see the larger picture and obtaining a lay of the property would definitely help solidify a plan of attack.

He rose to his feet. "Is the road to the main house clear?"

Startled, Lorenzo skuttled to his feet. "Yes, I walked it this morning."

"Is there a shortcut through the woods?" Nikolai pulled on his overcoat and hat.

"Of course. Beyond the barn is a trail that will take you there." He poured some hot liquid from the kettle next to the fire into an earthenware mug. "Careful, the path is narrow in some places."

With a nod, Nikolai stepped out into the cold. The chill revitalized him crystalizing a sense of purpose and familiarity in his mind. He circumvented the cottage and headed for the barn. Inside, the horses whickered and shuffled.

Behind the barn, he scanned the tree line for a gap wide enough for a trail. A snow-dusted bough hung across it. He ducked around it, careful not to disturb the snow. The trail was narrow, but he managed to follow the markings easily. If the ground were covered completely, then he could see how easily one could lose their way.

The trail spilled into a clearing beside a large manor house. Nikolai scoffed. How could this possibly be called a hunting lodge? The ostentatious building looked as though it had been plucked from a bustling metropolis such as Vienna or Paris and set in the middle of a forest. *A shame indeed.*

He took his time walking around the house and saw no signs betraying any recent visitors. All the shutters were drawn tight. No sound penetrated the dense forest surrounding the building. Yet what should have been a peaceful landscape lay eerie and uncomfortably still. Nikolai searched the trees and the mountains rising in the distance. Nothing seemed amiss, but the feeling persisted.

Turning up his collar, Nikolai wove back through the trees and emerged as the last rays of light settled behind the mountains casting the valley into deep shadows. He ensured the horses were fed and safely stowed before returning to the cottage.

When he opened the door, the overwhelming scent of the rabbit stew made his mouth water. He closed and locked the door behind him after he hung up his overcoat.

Lorenzo stood by the fire ladling food into a bowl. "You must be hungry."

Gertrude sat at the table with a bowl steaming between her hands. She pursed her lips and blew across the surface of the bowl, her lashes fluttering across her cheek.

Nikolai shifted uncomfortably at the desire such an innocent action conjured.

The groundskeeper handed him the bowl. "Sit. Eat."

Even as he sat, Gertrude did not meet his gaze. She remained focused on her meal. Spoonful by spoonful, she ate in silence without giving him so much as an acknowledgment.

Must she be so difficult? Even though he read her innermost thoughts and desires in the journal, she refused to betray even a glimpse of those emotions in his presence. Could this possibly be the same woman who wrote such passionate confessions?

Lorenzo joined them, offering a few pieces of crusty bread. "It may be meager fare, but it will fill your belly and stave off the cold."

The first bite tasted better than some of the more refined food he had in countess's employment. The meat fell off the bone, and the vegetables retained some firmness which he found he preferred to mush.

"It is delicious. Thank you." Gertrude smiled at the groundskeeper purposely avoiding meeting Nikolai's gaze and returning to her meal.

"Tomorrow I shall go to the village and retrieve more supplies." Lorenzo took a bite of stew. "How long are you planning on staying?"

"A week at the most," Nikolai replied between bites. "Unless our presence proves to be an inconvenience."

"Not at all." Lorenzo grinned dipping his bread into the broth. "It will be nice to have some company for a change. Since my wife passed, these hills have become far too lonely."

Gertrude pushed her spoon in the broth at the bottom of her bowl.

"I can pay you for supplies and for the accommodations." Nikolai offered trying to shift the melancholy conversation toward a more neutral topic.

The old man waved his hand. "While I appreciate the sentiment, a week of company is payment enough."

They finished their meal and cleaned what little mess they created. Lorenzo retired, leaving Gertrude and Nikolai alone in the main room.

She tensed as he approached her.

"This cottage is quite small." He brushed a piece of lint from her shoulder. "You cannot avoid me forever."

Gertrude spun around, her blue eyes sparkling like sapphires in the firelight. "You never told him we weren't married."

"No. I merely chose to not correct his assumption. There's a difference."

Her brow furrowed as the scowl deepened. "You expect me to play along with this charade?"

"I expect you to follow instructions." Her scent filled his head with wicked visions. "You came to my door after I gave specific instructions for you remain at the countess's estate."

"Only to deliver the letters." She propped her hands on her hips. "You threw me over your shoulder and practically carried me onto the train.”

Her point struck a firm blow. He clenched his hands into fists to keep from grabbing her by the shoulders and shaking her. “You should have followed my instructions.”

“Well, then how would you have received the letters?”

“I had every intention of returning to the estate.” He glowered. “If you would have remained there, none of this would have been necessary.”

“So, follow your orders and everything will be fine, is that it?”

The current between them sparked with energy much like the coils he saw in an article on a scientist named Tesla. Nikolai grit his teeth. “Do you know why the countess requested I work for her all those years ago?”

“Well, it was not for your sparkling wit and conversation.”

“Insolence does not become you, Gertrude. Do not make me put you over my knee.”

Her eyes widened and she hissed in a breath. “You would not dare lay a hand on me.”

“If you persist in behaving like a rebellious child, then I will treat you as one.” He enjoyed the way her breaths came quicker and her lips parted in shock. When she pressed her mouth into a thin line, he continued, “The countess hired me to ensure her safety and as well as those within her purview. This extends to you, whether you like it or not.”

“I would have been safe at the estate.”

“Yes, you would have, if you had not come to my apartment.”

Gertrude shook her head. “I do not understand.”

“When you left the house carrying those letters, you made yourself a target.” His voice softened a fraction. “I could not in good conscience allow you to remain in Vienna unprotected.”

She scoffed. “You have a conscience?”

“Believe what you want, *liebling*, but I am not as heartless as you believe me to be.” Exhaustion eroded what remained of his resolve. “Go to sleep. I will remain here.”

She opened her mouth as if to protest and snapped it closed

quickly. With a nod, Gertrude pushed past him and stalked up the stairs.

When he heard the soft thud of the door closing, Nikolai collapsed on the chair by the fire and buried his hands in his hair. Why in heaven did he fall in love with a woman more stubborn than himself? And what would it take for him to tell her the truth of his affection?

After five years in service to the countess, Gertrude longed for solitude and some time for reflection. But four days of being trapped under the same roof with Nikolai and having nothing to distract her from the constant awareness of his presence drove her close to madness.

On the fourth morning after their arrival, she woke alone in the oversized bed. Nikolai kept his promise, allowing her to have at least a small amount of privacy. Not that she worried he would take advantage of her. No, what worried her was her inability to stave off the hunger she contained efficiently for so long. Without her journal to purge the thoughts in her mind and the countess offering some form of distraction, she found Nikolai's presence even more of a temptation.

She rose from the bed and wrapped a cozy, patchwork blanket around her. Smoldering embers in the fireplace barely touched the chill. The frosted glass on the windows glowed with the morning light. The warm woolen slippers Lorenzo provided kept her feet from freezing. He also provided some of his wife's old garments for her use. His thoughtfulness warmed her heart.

Her stomach growled. Carefully she descended the stairs and the warmth of the fireplace surrounded her. A hearty blaze roared in the hearth and the smell of coffee filled the air.

In the large chair beside the fire, Nikolai sat asleep. His head lay tucked against his shoulder, his legs extended and propped on a small stool. Anson's journal pressed open against his chest tucked beneath his crossed arms. Her heart softened at the sight of his expression relaxed in sleep.

Lorenzo appeared beside her.

"Good morning," he whispered. "Seems your husband fell asleep reading again last eve." He chuckled.

"Yes." She dropped her gaze to the man who stole her heart, even in sleep.

"There is coffee beside the fire, and I placed some porridge in the pot to warm. The honey is in the pantry." He winked.

"Thank you." Gertrude smiled.

The groundskeeper nodded. "I shall return later. I must check the property."

Alarm spread through her. "Why? Has something happened?"

"It snowed quite a bit last night while we all slept." He grabbed his coat by the door and bundled himself up. "I must ensure nothing was damaged and the horses are fed. Not to worry."

Gertrude watched him leave, noting the vast expanse of white outside as he slipped out into the cold morning. She peered through the window, wiping the frost off with the blanket corner.

The tree boughs pulled down heavy with snow. The snow-covered ground reflected the muted sunlight through the clouds. A beautiful, pristine scene lay beyond the window, begging for exploration. Perhaps she could enjoy it after breakfast.

She quietly poured herself some coffee and ladled some porridge into a bowl. Her gaze drifted to the man slumbering to her left. Once she set the bowl aside, she crept closer to his side.

His lashes lay softly fanned against his cheek. The age lines at the corners of his eyes and between his brows were smoothed by the comforting embrace of sleep. He looked much younger, but still devastatingly handsome. Her fingers itched to run through his gray flecked hair.

In all the time she had known him, she had never seen him in such a peaceful state. There were times she wondered if he ever slept at all, considering he always seemed to be present. A true shadow, in all sense of the words, and yet her heart ached for him.

He spoke briefly of his past on the train, but she heard the unspoken words as clearly as those he shared. His work was his life. Nothing else mattered.

The urge overcame her once more. Daring fate, she reached out and brushed her fingers over his temple, threading her fingertips through his hair. So soft. She repeated the motion.

Nikolai's hand shot up from where it rested against his chest and grasped her wrist.

She gasped, her heart thundering like a hundred horses galloping across a field.

His jade eyes fixed on her while his body slowly unraveled from sleep.

"I...uh, you had something in your hair." She fumbled with the words knowing exactly how weak her reasoning sounded.

"How kind of you to address it." He tugged her wrist and she stumbled back falling directly into his lap. The journal slid to the floor with a thud, but his attention remained focused on her. Both arms wrapped around her, holding her firmly across his muscular thighs.

"What are you doing?" She squirmed trying to free herself. "Release me."

His grip only tightened. "Stop moving, woman." His guttural command sent a sensation of need spiraling straight to her core.

Gertrude stilled. "Please, Nikolai." Her plea transcended both desires. While her mind demanded she run away from him, her heart pleaded for him to pull her closer, to take what he desired and end her torture. But he made it apparent he did not want her in this way.

Their eyes locked in a silent exchange. She could read nothing except her body's own response to him. Gradually, his grip loosened.

She rose from his lap and gathered the blanket from the floor.

Nikolai's jaw clenched, his gaze raked over her from head to foot.

Only then did she realize her state of undress. The worn

nightgown was practically sheer in the morning light. With a yelp, she wrapped the blanket around her and retreated up the stairs. Mortification stung her cheeks with heat.

Quickly, she dressed, being sure to wear a layer of warm stockings and skirts in order to venture out into the snow. Even though she tried to put the incident from her mind, it haunted her replaying over and over. How could she have been so selfish and forward. He looked ready to murder her for daring to touch him.

When she returned downstairs, Nikolai sat at the table with a bowl of porridge and a steaming mug of coffee. Gertrude attempted to fetch hers from the hearth, only to find it sitting across from Nikolai at the table.

Without a word, she sat. Silence gathered around them while they ate, until she could no longer take the stillness threatening to choke her.

"Did you find anything of importance in the major's journal?" Gertrude sipped her coffee.

"Nothing I did not already know." He leaned back in his chair and studied her.

"I should have returned it." Gertrude lamented with a pang of guilt.

"Perhaps you wished to protect me." He smirked. "Although admirable, my past is not a secret to anyone who knows where to search or whom to question."

She scoffed. "You wish me to believe you have no secrets to hide?"

"On the contrary." He tapped his finger on the mug. "I have many secrets."

Exasperated, Gertrude shook her head. "Must you always speak in riddles?"

He shrugged his shoulder. "I cannot change who I am."

His responses fanned the already burgeoning flames of frustration. "I should have returned the journal and left you to fend for yourself in Vienna."

"You are quite stunning when you become passionate." He leaned forward, placing his elbows on the table. A smirk played upon his lips.

Gertrude's face warmed. Was that a backhanded compliment? "You are quite infuriating when you play these games."

Nikolai tisked. "No games. Especially not with you, *liebling*." He rose to his feet. "Come."

Confused by the twisted meaning in his words and the way he softened toward her over the past few days, Gertrude followed him but maintained a good distance between them. They donned their winter outerwear and boots.

When she stepped out into the snow, a sense of freedom and wonder filtered deep into her soul. The quiet beauty drew her deeper into its enthrall. She stepped into the snow, surprised it came nearly to her knees.

She jumped back onto the safety of the porch and shook the wet powder from her legs.

Nikolai handed her a shovel and took one for himself. Together they hewed out a rough path to the barn using Lorenzo's footprints from earlier as a guide.

The exertion brought a sheen of sweat to his brow. Gertrude wiped her own and leaned against the barn.

"I forgot how much work there is to be done when there are no servants." She opened the top buttons of her cloak and let the cool air soothe her heated skin.

"Are you saying you have become soft?" Nikolai teased.

"Soft? No. Complacent? Yes." She admired the mountains rising in the distance.

When she glanced at him, her heart fluttered in her chest. Nikolai stood out, dark and stern against the white background. Handsome, almost regal, in bearing. Had she not known him, she would have assumed he belonged to a royal court or a noble household. The thought alone made her laugh.

Her laugh caught his attention and his gaze narrowed. "What amuses you?"

"What? Am I not allowed to laugh in your presence?"

"I do not think I have ever heard you laugh in such a way." His voice echoed between them.

The laughter died in her throat. "What do you mean? I laugh quite frequently."

"Not like that."

"Like what?" Curiosity burned through her like a wildfire. But the intensity of his gaze stoked it even hotter.

He inhaled deeply, staring off into the distance for a moment before facing her again. "Like you are unbound by ridiculous notions of society and constraint." His eyes brightened. "It sounds like the clearest bells ringing in joyful celebration."

Gertrude could not believe the words, but she heard the sincerity in his voice. Her cheeks heated and a tart reply withered on her lips.

Nikolai set his shovel on his shoulder and walked back to the house. The path made it easier to follow him, but she stumbled and toppled into the snow as they reached the cottage.

She struggled to right herself, and snow fell against her bare skin making her shiver. A strong arm wrapped around her waist and drew her from the snowbank. She stiffened when her body pressed against his. The overwhelming heat poured off his large frame and quelled the chill instantly.

He set her on the steps of the cottage and brushed off her skirts. When he straightened, she wobbled but he caught her with his steady hand.

"Go inside and warm yourself."

Gertrude longed to reach up and brush her fingers along his stubble roughened jaw. What would it be like to feel it against her skin when he kissed her? Would he return the kiss? Or would he push her away?

Before she could bolster her courage, he stepped back and turned, heading toward the barn once more. She cursed herself a coward and stalked into the cottage.

Inside, she collapsed in a chair beside the fire and hung her head. Why could she not commit to action when it came to Nikolai? His sudden change in demeanor left her with a torrent of conflicting emotions. Where once he was cold and distant, he now left her wondering if he truly cared for her?

Frustrated, she kicked the chair across from her. The journal he had been reading earlier tumbled to the floor from beneath a blanket. She picked it up to replace it but instead sat down and opened the pages, wondering if she could uncover anything more from within its depths.

Her breath caught, and a thousand thoughts collided inside her mind. The words in the journal were not in English. They were German. They were her words.

Nikolai found her journal.

This meant nothing. Nikolai only spoke a few words of German. He never studied her language, therefore the secrets contained within were still safe.

But why had it been in his hands this morning?

Gertrude searched the room, hoping to find Anson's journal, but found nothing.

"Mein Gott in Himmel."

The door opened behind her. Startled, Gertrude tucked the journal in the folds of her skirt and sat down. She closed her eyes and prayed.

Chapter Nine

No distance seemed to be enough to quell the pull between them. Nikolai prayed the cold would ease his agony, but it only enflamed it. He had been a fool to touch her and underestimate the powerful connection which bound him to her.

Stepping inside the cottage, he half expected her to be tucked in her room upstairs, hidden away from him. He closed the door and hung his coat on the wall. When he found her sitting in front of the fire with her hands demurely in her lap, he paused wondering if she were lost in thought and had not heard him enter the cottage.

No. Something was wrong. Loosening his shirt at the collar, he stepped closer. To anyone else, Gertrude would seem composed and peaceful. But Nikolai knew her too well. Her fingertips fluttered against the fabric of her skirts. Her crystalline gaze drawn deep into the flames.

He sat in the chair opposite, expecting her to startle at his appearance. Yet she remained steadfast.

Her lips pursed tighter at his scrutiny. "It is impolite to stare."

Nikolai rested his elbow on the arm of the chair and leaned his jaw against his palm. He maintained his steady perusal of her expression.

The indifference melted into agitation, until finally she faced him.

"Do you intend to stare at me all day?" Her jaw hardened.

"Am I not permitted to admire your beauty?" He pressed, hoping to soften her demeanor and see a flush of need blossom in her eyes once more. He glimpsed it earlier, but he knew one taste and he would not be able to restrain his desires.

Her lip trembled. "Do not tease me, Nikolai. I am in no

mood for your games."

"Do you find my attentions so repulsive?" He softened his voice as though attempting to soothe a skittish filly.

Gertrude's eyes drifted closed. "Don't."

He moved closer, kneeling on the floor beside her. When his fingers brushed the bare skin on the back of her hand, her eyes flew wide and she jumped to her feet twisting out of his reach.

Something hit the floor between them. Gertrude gasped and stooped to pick it up, clutching it to her chest.

Her journal.

She found it. It mattered not how she discovered it, for now the truth lay bare between them. A weight lifted from his conscience when he met her soulful gaze.

"You found your journal." He rose to his feet and stepped closer.

"Yes." For every step which brought him closer, she retreated in kind. The book clutched to her breast like a shield between them. "Did you take it? On the train?"

Nikolai shook his head slowly. "I found it in the dining car."

She continued her retreat determined to remain out of reach. He tempered down the surge of predatory glee threatening to burst forth. It would only frighten her. Instead, he stalked her with measured steps. Give and take. A cat toying with an extremely delightful mouse.

"Why did you not return it?" Her voice trembled, but she tipped her chin up meeting his gaze squarely.

"I was not finished reading it." His confession made her stumble.

"You read it?" She caught herself quickly and rounded the table. "You speak German? I did not know you spoke it."

"*Liebling*, there is much you do not know about me." He followed her.

She swayed. He leapt forward to catch her, but she darted past him back toward the hearth.

While he relished their little game, his patience began to wear quite thin.

"You read my journal. You kept it from me." She glared at him.

Nikolai found her words amusing. "Tell me the truth, *liebling*." He crossed the room with gentle steps. "The words in your journal tell a much different story."

"Do not mock me." She inhaled deeply.

"It was never my intention to deceive you." He stood nearly an arm's length from her. "When I discovered your journal, I meant to return it. But when I saw what it contained." He groaned in pleasure. "I could not relinquish such a jewel."

Gertrude's mouth fell open, and a soft gasp escaped her lips. Nikolai seized his opportunity and wrapped his hand around her wrist. He pulled her against him, settling her against his body. Her warmth infused him as it had this morning when he pulled her down into his lap. He wanted to kiss her then, but something, perhaps a tug of conscience, kept his resolve strong.

She writhed in effort to free herself. "Release me."

"No. For too long I have denied myself." He tightened his hold, her luscious curves molding to his body. She stilled, but he held firm.

Their breaths synchronized. He felt the wild beating of her heart against his chest.

"Denied yourself?" She tipped her head back to meet his gaze. "What do you mean?"

For years he dreamt of this moment, his opportunity to unveil his heart to her. And yet his voice failed him. Nikolai, soldier and member of the secret police, guardian and protector, could not confess his affection. A barrel of a gun would be more welcome than the sapphire gaze of the woman he loved.

Instead of relying on words, Nikolai captured her mouth in a kiss as tender as it was desperate. She tensed for a moment but softened the moment he deepened the kiss, tasting her. She writhed against him. Her journal dropped to the floor.

She wrapped her arms around him.

In all his years, Nikolai never came close to feeling true contentment. Holding her in his embrace, he finally felt a sense of peace in his distant soul. A soul he once thought he traded away on a whim. The taste and scent of her teased him beyond redemption. He clung tighter, unwilling to relinquish her after such an arduous struggle.

"Nikolai." His name on her tongue soothed like a healing balm and stung like the bite of a saber blade.

"*Liebling*." He drew back enough to savor the blush of passion staining her lovely face. "I have wanted this from the first moment I saw you."

"What is this madness?" Her grip on his shirt tightened. She licked her lips, searching his face for affirmation of his honesty. "For years you tormented me with your presence. At every turn, you harassed and belittled me, treating me like a child with no mind of my own. I should hate you for the years I spent in agony over this unrelenting affection that held you so dear to my heart."

"I can offer no apology to ease the pain my actions brought upon you." His eyes drifted shut and spoke from the depths of his soul. "Forgive me, *liebling*."

"You cannot ask me to forgive your actions."

Despair gutted him at her words. "I have no defense. Those actions and my confession hold two halves of the same truth. My need for you superseded my reason. For that, I apologize."

She cupped his cheek in her palm. The simple touch reignited the fire her kiss brought to life. "For all the romantic advice we offered the major and Matilda, still we could not face our own internal struggle with affection."

"Strange how simple it is to offer advice, and yet we are not wise enough apply it to our own lives." He kissed her tenderly, drawing a soft mewl from deep in her throat. "Actions do speak louder than words, do they not?"

"Perhaps we have been remiss in our past behavior. I should like to remedy that." She threaded her fingers through his hair and pulled him in for another passionate kiss.

Nikolai growled and lifted her off the ground. She laughed, squirming as carried her to the chair and sat with her settled upon his lap. He tugged the shawl tucked into her bodice. It fell away revealing the voluptuous curve of her breasts. He brushed his cheek against them inhaling the sweet scent of her skin.

She moaned and tangled her hands in his hair. "Nikolai, *bitte.*"

He raked his teeth across her delicate skin, leaving her gasping and writhing in his lap. With nimble fingers, he unlaced her bodice and tugged it down, revealing a pair of glorious orbs with bright rosy nipples. He cupped one in his palm and savored the weight of it in his hand. His fingertips rolled the taut nipple.

Gertrude moaned and buried her face in his neck. Her hands fisted in the fabric of his shirt.

He shifted her in his lap, draping her leg over the arm of the chair. Gently, he trailed his fingertips along her calf and up beneath her skirts.

"Once I brand you, *liebling,* you belong to me," he whispered against her hair.

Nothing save the hand of God himself could stop him from claiming her. Gertrude would be his until the stars fell from the sky.

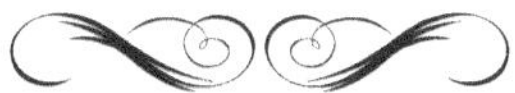

Desire burned through her, hotter and brighter than anything she experienced in her life. When she realized Nikolai read her journal, she feared the worst, but this proved more than she ever hoped for.

She clung tightly to him as he lay siege to her body. With a touch more tender than she expected, he drew out her pleasure making her moan and beg like a wanton whore. Even her husband had not released this much passion when he took her.

His hand stilled beneath her skirts. "Once I brand you, *liebling,* you belong to me."

Nikolai's manhood pressed firmly against her hip. It seemed she wielded as much power over him as he did over her. She wiggled in his lap, making him growl. His steel grip on her thigh made her cease her teasing.

"Would you rather I stop?" He withdrew his hand.

"No." She grasped his hand and held it to her thigh.

"You like to misbehave." The pressure intensified again as

he trailed his hand higher. "Perhaps I should bend you over my knee. Hmmm?"

Gertrude whimpered at the thought.

"Does that excite you?" He nuzzled her ear, drawing the lobe between his teeth. "The thought of my hand leaving marks on your backside. A reminder for you to behave."

She nodded, unable to trust her voice.

His hand cupped her sex. Her skirts lay bunched around her waist. Her gaze flitted to the door. Should Lorenzo return, he would see her splayed across Nikolai's lap, dazed with sexual fervor desperate for release. The thought alone only increased her excitement.

Nikolai slid his finger into the slit of her drawers. She winced at the slick sounds filling the silent room as he touched her.

"*Liebling.*" He delved deeper, his fingers playing over her sex with the talent of a master tuning his instrument.

She bucked against his hand. Unimaginable sensations coursing through her with every stroke of his dexterous fingers. She never thought such pleasure could be wrought in such a way. He played on, moving and sliding, creating music in the form of the vibration humming through her.

"Yes, *liebling.*" He kissed her cheek and quickened the tempo.

Gertrude grasped the arm of the chair with one hand and Nikolai's shirt with the other. Her body pulsed in waves as a blissful sensation peaked and receded leaving her elated and exhausted.

Nikolai pulled her skirts down and cradled her in his arms. She nestled against him, and for the first time in years, a contented calm settled over her.

"Had I known you were so sensitive, *liebling,* I would have seduced you years ago."

"I wish you had." She tipped her head back. Those enigmatic jade eyes drew her into their depths. "Will you make love to me now?"

He raised a brow in question. "Later. First rest, let us enjoy the moment."

She rested her head against him and sighed. Her eyes grew heavy and the edges of the room faded into darkness. She closed them knowing she was safe in Nikolai's embrace.

A loud bang woke her with a start. She startled, and Nikolai's arms tightened around her.

"Oh, there you are." Lorenzo stumbled into the door. "Looks like there is another storm coming."

Nikolai shifted Gertrude on his lap. She quickly readjusted her bodice and tied it before turning back to Lorenzo. When she tried to stand, Nikolai refused to release her. She kissed his jaw and the tension in his arms eased. Finally, he relinquished his hold.

She stood and brushed out her skirts. "I am glad you returned before the storm arrived."

"So am I, my dear." The old groundskeeper hung up his coat and bustled toward the fire to warm his hands.

"Let me make you something hot to drink." Gertrude set to work, ladling some water into the kettle and hanging it over the fire.

As she worked, her attention drifted to Nikolai who remained in the chair. His focus lay solely on her. The intensity of it nearly made her spill the tin containing the tea leaves.

He brushed his hand over his mouth, hiding the beginning of a smile. As if she needed a reminder of his hands and his wicked mouth. He teased her more, drawing his lower lip between his teeth.

Gertrude's face heated. She placed the tea into the mugs and waited for the water to heat.

After a few minutes, she offered tea to Nikolai and Lorenzo, who accepted it with gusto. She sat on the stool beside Nikolai and blew across the surface of the mug before taking a sip.

Lorenzo graced them with a story featuring one of the legends of the area. Gertrude was familiar with the tale and smiled at the telling. She became lost in the memories it brought back of her own childhood outside of Munich.

A loud knock on the door shook the cottage. Lorenzo and

Nikolai both shot to their feet.

"Did you see anyone while you were out?" Nikolai asked the groundskeeper.

"No one. Not even tracks." Lorenzo reached for his rifle next to the door.

Nikolai drew his pistol and turned toward her. "Go upstairs. Lock the door. Whatever you hear, do not come down until I tell you." Gone was the loving man who brought her pleasure, replaced with the hard, calculated soldier who stood sentry for his whole life.

Gertrude nodded unaware of what else she could say to convince him of her safety. She kissed him and darted up the stairs.

Once she locked the door, Gertrude grabbed a blanket off the bed and hid in the wardrobe, using it to both shield her and keep her warm. The sound of raised voices echoed through the floorboards.

Finally, the door slammed and silence fell.

A soft knocking came filtering through the wardrobe. She cracked the cabinet and peered at the door leading downstairs. The knock came again.

"They have gone." Lorenzo's voice came through the wood. "It is safe to come out."

Gertrude unfurled herself from her hiding place and rushed down the stairs. But her elation faded when Nikolai's presence was notably absent.

"Where is he?"

"Your husband?" Lorenzo offered a comforting smile. "The innkeeper's son arrived demanding he accompany him."

"Where did they go?" she asked, fear rising in her gut.

"To the village inn most likely. Said something about needing to discuss some unfinished business."

A lump of dread threatened to choke her. Gertrude nodded, unable to think. Did this have something to do with the letters he received? Or was it only the innkeeper's son demanding he pay more for the horse they rented from the inn's stables? There were far too many unanswered questions.

She stared at the door hoping it would swing open and Nikolai would return. She only wished she had demanded an explanation of this whole mess earlier, but her desire distracted her. Being in his arms filled a dream she long thought would remain unfulfilled.

"Come, my dear. Sit with me while I make some venison stew." Lorenzo motioned to the chair sitting by the table.

"Perhaps I should check..."

"The snow has already begun to fall. It would be wise for you to wait here. I am sure a strapping lad like him will be fine. He will return in no time. You will see." The groundskeeper pulled out a knife and cut up the meat, tossing it in the pot.

Gertrude, torn with indecision, relented and helped prepare the stew.

After they had both eaten, Lorenzo insisted she sleep. But she could find no peace.

Gertrude sat in the chair by the hearth huddled beneath the blanket, her attention fixed on the door. Sounds, like the crack of an axe splitting firewood, echoed outside in the darkness. Fear coiled in her gut making her nauseated. She could not shake the suspicion something had happened. Something horrible.

"Lorenzo?" She knocked on his door.

He appeared, fully dressed. "Yes, I heard it too. Could be snow falling from the rooftop." He patted her hand. "Do not worry. I will investigate."

"Thank you." While it did not ensure Nikolai's safety, she found it easier to rest knowing the older man would protect her without hesitation. He disappeared into the night, leaving her with the specific instructions to return to bed, lock the door, and rest.

The snowstorm intensified, and darkness lay foreboding beyond the white curtain outside. Whatever happened, her search would have to wait until morning.

Gertrude prayed it would not come to that. He would return. He always did.

He dies. The words in the letter haunted her.

Nikolai, where are you?

Chapter Ten

A heavy curtain of snow fell from the heavens blocking everything more than several steps ahead. The innkeeper's son led the way through the darkness, his lantern swaying like a beacon. Nikolai squinted against the flakes as they pelted his face and pulled his coat tight, keeping a firm grip on the pistol in his pocket.

The moment the innkeeper's son appeared at the door Nikolai felt the hair on the back of his neck rise. More than half his life spent between the military and the Okhrana gave him a keen sense of awareness.

When he requested Nikolai return to the village in the middle of a storm, the stench of betrayal lingered behind the young man's nervous request. The time had come.

At least Gertrude remained securely hidden. He followed the young man hoping whomever hired him chose a meeting place away from the cottage.

They wove along the path he and Matilda carved earlier toward the barn.

"You can retrieve your horse and follow me into town." The young man paused outside the barn. A shaft of the lantern's light illuminated his face. His gaze remained fixed in the distance, his lips pressed tightly together. Nikolai grasped understanding immediately. *Fear.*

Gripping the pistol tighter, he nodded and opened the barn door.

The musty smell of hay and horse manure clung to the air. He allowed himself a moment for his eyes to adjust to the darkness. With little light to assist him, Nikolai stepped inside out of the storm.

Silence greeted him like a warm friend. He drew his pistol

keeping it tucked to his side. No soft shuffling of horse hooves in hay or the gentle whickers demanding food. The horses were gone. *Shit.*

Nikolai pressed his back against the wall and slid deeper into the shadows. "Come out."

A soft chuckle filtered through the stale air followed by the broken Russian of a man unfamiliar with Nikolai's mother tongue. "You are better than they claimed."

The tell-tale hiss of a match strike and a tiny pin prick of light filled the space. A lantern glowed to life, revealing two men standing beside the nearest stall. One held the light while the other pointed a gun directly at Nikolai.

"Put the gun down before you hurt yourself." The man with the pistol stepped closer switching to English with a hint of an unfamiliar accent.

Jaw clenched, Nikolai carefully tossed his gun to the ground and lifted his hands into view. His mind spun into action. Two men plus the innkeeper's son, who could merely be a pawn. One gun, but if there was one, there were more concealed. He weighed his odds and found them satisfactory.

"Ah, before you make any rash decisions—" the gunman glared at him "—consider the position in which you find yourself." A sadistic smile tugged at his mouth. "One whisper of trouble, and the innkeeper's boy has orders to torch the cottage with your lovely whore inside."

Blood rushed through his veins igniting a dark corner of his soul. "If you so much as harm a single hair on her head, I will rip your throat out with my teeth and watch you drown in your own filth."

The man's brow arched. "You are hardly in a position to make demands."

He lifted a shoulder in response. No words would reach through the man's shortsightedness. Nikolai instead focused on his plan of attack.

The gunman whistled. From the darkness, shadows unveiled themselves. One. Two. Three. *Fuck.* Four. Five. As he counted, the men stepped into the lantern light. Each of them armed. A pack of murderous thugs salivating like a pack of wild dogs on the scent of blood.

"Underestimating the infamous Nikolai Voronia would have been an unforgivable mistake." The gunman grinned. "Tie him up boys. Once you have him, fetch his whore."

Nikolai ground his teeth. His life he forfeit long ago, but Gertrude belonged to him.

"If you touch her, I will not only kill you and your families, but I will burn it all to ashes and spit on your corpses." Nikolai's voice dropped in warning.

The gunman's smile dissolved and he snatched the lantern from the man beside him. "Gag him as well."

Six men advanced. Nikolai stepped away from the wall, enough to give him room for the incoming scuffle. They could not shoot him without injuring one of their own men, so he used it to his advantage.

The first man grabbed for Nikolai's arm. He ducked out of reach and swung his fist. The crunch of his knuckles hitting the man's jaw echoed like a swan song in his head. Pushing away hesitation, Nikolai allowed the bloodlust to flow.

One by one, they came at him grabbing at his arms, his legs, anything they could. Nikolai danced out of reach, landing blow after blow until finally they changed tactics.

Instead of trying to subdue him, they fought back. A crack to the side of his head diverted his attention from the impact of one of their fists to his side. He braced against the blow and spun around, tossing them backwards.

While one swung at his face, another jumped on his back trying to pin him down with sheer weight. Nikolai threw a right hook, knocking the first one to the floor and then leveraged his body enough to toss the brute clinging to his back over his shoulder. He landed with a thud on the one scrambling to get back to his feet. The two men lay in a heap and did not move.

Two more stepped in to fill the void. One grabbed Nikolai's arm while the other landed a punch in his gut. Nikolai grabbed him by the throat and rammed his head into the second man, knocking them both to the ground.

He spun in time for the force of another fist to collide with his face. A warm trickle of blood ran down his cheek. He stumbled back and then drove head first toward the man who had dealt the blow.

They both tumbled to the floor. Nikolai seized a handful of hair and slammed his head down onto the cold, hard dirt.

The cocking of a pistol made him freeze halfway upon standing.

"Impressive. Perhaps I did underestimate you after all."

Nikolai straightened to his full height, carefully sliding his hand along the inside of his calf under the pretense of bracing himself, and surveyed the damage he wrought. Five men lay sprawled across the floor. The remaining two cowered behind the leader who held the pistol steady. Nikolai kept his hands at his sides.

Blood dripped from the cut above his eye. His lip ached. He licked the split bisecting his lower lip, savoring the metallic tang on his tongue.

"Why send in the dogs when you can shoot me?" Nikolai smirked, the action making his lip sting. "Kill me and be done with it."

The man tisked. "I would. Gladly. But my orders are to subdue you, not kill you."

"Your orders?" Nikolai scoffed and spit a mouthful of saliva and blood. "Hired thugs."

"No, Mr. Voronia, we are not hired thugs. We are professionals tasked with explicit instructions to subdue you, with any force necessary."

"Why?" He shrugged. "Surely your employer wants me dead. Why waste time and effort?" He narrowed his gaze. "Shoot me."

"If it were that simple, I would love to do the deed myself." The gunman sighed. "Alas, there are unanswered questions which much be addressed before I put a bullet between your eyes."

"Ask the questions and get on with it." Nikolai taunted the man, and the two flanking him relaxed sharing a cocky smirk.

They stepped out from behind their leader and crossed their arms.

"Impatient to die, are you, Mr. Voronia?" The man laughed.

"No, just waiting for the perfect opportunity." Nikolai took a deep breath to steady himself.

"The perfect opportunity for what?" The gunman laughed harder. "To escape? Who said you have no sense of humor?"

"To kill you." Nikolai registered the look of shock on their faces when he raised a small pistol and pulled the trigger once, twice, three times. A bullet for each man, directly between the eyes. The lantern clattered against the cold dirt, and three thugs crumbled in a massive heap.

Nikolai picked up the lantern and hung it on the post. Then he gathered some rope and unsheathed the knife from inside his other boot. He dragged the unconscious men into the first stall and bound each of them, one to the other ensuring none of them would escape unless they worked as a team. He grinned to himself. A crew like this had nothing but their own self-interest at heart. They were his prisoners.

He cracked the door, noting the innkeeper's son had long since disappeared. Damn. Honestly, he was not concerned about the local innkeeper's son. Not yet, at least. He would send the groundskeeper to the village for help as soon as he uncovered the truth behind this little unsuccessful abduction.

One by one, Nikolai pulled the three dead men to the side of the room lining them up side by side. Beside the small stall, he found a chair which he placed in the center of the floor.

Untying one man, he dragged him across the manure strewn stall and propped him in the chair and tied him fast. His unconscious head hung down against his chest. This would never do.

Nikolai picked up a small bucket of ice-cold water from the horses' stall and poured it over the bound man's head.

"Oi. What!" The man shot awake, ripping at his bonds trying to escape the icy rivulets now cascading over his filthy hair and torn clothes. He shook his head to get the hair out of his eyes. When he noticed Nikolai, he glowered and spit.

"The last three were unhelpful." Nikolai removed his coat and draped it over the stall door. He rolled his sleeves slowly basking in the chill and the heat roiling through his veins. "Perhaps you can offer something more useful."

"Fuck off, Russian pig." He spit again.

Nikolai grasped the man's hair and held his head back, their gazes locked in silent battle. "If you refuse to answer my questions, then I will torture you until you do. Then, and only then, will I show mercy and end your suffering."

"You might as well kill me. I will tell you nothing."

Nikolai nodded. "Very well." He placed the blade of his knife to the man's throat and smiled at the startled gasp at the press of the blade against cold flesh. "For every time you do not answer, I remove a piece of you."

The man trembled. "You would never."

"You have no idea what I would or would not do." Nikolai remained impassive even though his heart thundered against his aching ribs. "Are you willing to play roulette?"

"Fuck you, Russian bastard."

Nikolai trailed the knife along the squirming man's jaw and notched it to the gap below his ear. "One last chance. Tell me. Or I will take your ears, then a finger, then a toe, alternating until I finally resort to cutting off your cock and balls." He grinned at the horror emblazoned on the man's face. "Or would you rather I start with those? Seems only fitting to castrate you filthy mongrels."

The sharp edge nicked the skin causing a rivulet of blood to run down the cur's neck.

"Fine. It was some Frenchman. He hired us to follow you. Once we knew you were alone, we were to nab you and take you to meet the bloke who hired us."

"The Frenchman, does he have a name?" Nikolai applied some more pressure.

The man hissed and gestured to the dead gunman. "He was the one who spoke to him, did all the negotiating. I don't know any details. I swear."

Nikolai eased the knife away. "Do any of your other

companions have this information?"

He shook his head. "Maybe. I doubt it. Why don't you threaten them and see what they tell you?"

Nikolai smiled, baring his teeth in a feral way. "Oh, I intend to do just that."

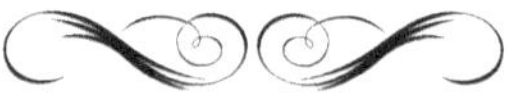

An endless night of tossing and turning left Gertrude exhausted. She shivered at the biting chill in the room. The coals burned low in the gate smoldering into embers. At first, she considered rebuilding the fire and attempting to sleep, but all thoughts of this dissipated as the fog lifted from her mind. *Nikolai.*

She climbed from beneath a mountain of blankets and wrapped one around her shoulders. Then she pulled on a pair of warm slippers and rushed down the stairs.

A warm fire burned in the hearth and the lingering scent of coffee hung in the air.

"Lorenzo?" She searched the cottage for the groundskeeper and Nikolai but found neither.

Gertrude ran to the window and brushed the frost off the pane. Outside the world lay enveloped in white. Even the path they made the day before lay completely covered.

Lorenzo had promised to investigate the noise last night. Had he not returned? Gertrude's guilt at sending him out into a blizzard twisted in the pit of her stomach. Something happened. It must have.

Determined to uncover the mystery, Gertrude returned upstairs, donned her warmest garments, as well as warm winter gear Lorenzo had provided, and ventured out into the winter landscape.

The world, covered in white, lay undisturbed and still. A few lazy snowflakes drifted from the gray sky. She pulled her cloak tighter, burrowing beneath the hood to block out the chill. The boots protected her feet from the snow but her skirts soaked up the damp flakes with every step.

She wandered around the cottage, searching for any sign of Nikolai or Lorenzo. When she approached the barn, a noise made her pause. A man's voice? She crept closer to the barn. The voice grew louder and more distinct.

Nikolai. Relief flooded her. He was safe. She reached for the barn door latch when a man's scream tore through the air.

She froze, her hand resting on the latch. Nikolai spoke again. She could not make out the words with his strong accent, but the intensity of his voice both drew her curiosity and repelled her.

Quietly, she pushed open the barn door. Nikolai stood with his back to her, his broad shoulders filling her view completely.

Another scream ripped through to her very soul. Nikolai stepped to the side, revealing a man seated in a chair. Blood dripped down his face over his blackened and swollen eye. Her gaze drifted over him to the masses lying at Nikolai's feet. Bodies. Some writhed and groaned, while others lay unnaturally still. They were dead.

Gertrude stifled a scream behind her gloved hand. Her wide eyes flew to Nikolai who spun around at the sound. Blood smeared his handsome face. It blended and caked in the hair at his temples. His eyes alight with unharnessed aggression softened upon meeting hers.

Never in all her days could she have envisioned Nikolai in such a manner, drenched in blood and fury. Avenging angel or ravaging demon. Both warring factions existing side-by-side seemed impossible, and yet this described Nikolai in completion.

"*Liebling.*" His tender voice cut through the haze and surrounding gore.

With a shake of her head, Gertrude whirled around and raced back toward the cottage, away from the stench of blood and death. Away from the man, no, the monster she thought she loved. She stumbled through the snow drifts and tripped, tumbling forward into a pile of powder soft snow.

As she struggled to right herself, a warm pair of hands wrapped around hers and pulled. Nikolai, wearing no coat and no gloves, lifted her effortlessly to her feet. Once she found her bearing, she wrenched her hands from his.

"*Liebling,*" he began, but she held up her hand to silence him.

"No." She shook her head vehemently. "Do not call me that." Her gaze drifted back to the barn stark against the forest behind him. "What have you done? Are they dead?"

His expression hardened, and yet his reply seemed controlled, almost diplomatic. "Would you rather I let them kill me and then have their way with you?" Nikolai stepped closer, his breath forming whisps of smoke as though he were about to breathe fire and burn those who opposed him.

"Of course not." She met his gaze boldly. The stark contrast of the pristine landscape and the blood-soaked, disheveled Nikolai confounded her mind. It lay before her like a private glimpse inside the mind of a tormented man.

He swiped his hand across his brow and a fresh smear of crimson coated his forehead.

Gertrude gasped. "You are wounded."

A tired smirk pulled at the corners of his mouth.

She cleared her throat. "Come inside. Let me clean it."

Nikolai glanced back at the barn before nodding. "Give me a moment." Without waiting for her protest, he turned and strode back to the building.

Shouts and curses echoed from the open door. Curiosity nearly drove Gertrude to return and peer inside, but she did not think she could stomach the stench or the incomprehensible scene she witnessed moments before.

Gertrude retreated back to the cottage and peeled off the warm winter layers, hanging them to dry next to the fire. She put a kettle on the fire to heat water and retrieved some bandages and a small medical kit from the cabinet in the kitchen.

Upstairs in her room, she found a small sewing basket with thread and needles. There was no way to know if he would need stitches or not until she cleaned his wounds.

Her heart twisted with an attack of conscience. Seeing him in such a way tormented her and introduced a moral dilemma. She cared for him. Even after discovering the truth of his past in the pages of the major's journal and from his own lips, she cared for Nikolai deeply. He never claimed to be a saint or a gentleman. The countess would not have hired him had he not been efficient and competent in his abilities.

One has an ability to overlook the consequences of said abilities when they remain in the shadows. But for Gertrude, this proved to no longer be the case.

Nikolai was not evil, and his actions, monstrous as they seemed, were necessary. At least he believed so.

Gertrude bit her lip and hurried back down to pour some water in a basin and soak a rag. She searched the cabinets for some liquor.

The door swung open and hear heart nearly stopped. Nikolai entered the cottage and closed the door behind him. He hung his dirty overcoat by the door and sat on the bench next to the wall to pull off his boots.

"Where is Lorenzo?" she asked, rising to her full height.

"I sent him to the village to notify the authorities shortly after dawn." He glanced up at her approach. Lines of exhaustion creased his brow and settled deep at the corners of his eyes hidden by layers of blood and dirt.

Gertrude nodded. At least he was safe.

"Sit by the fire." She positioned the chair for the best light and tapped the back of it. She held her hand up before he sat. "Remove your clothes."

His brow raised in question.

Gertrude's face heated but she shook the embarrassment away. "I need to check for injuries and clean them."

Nikolai obliged without a word of protest. He unbuttoned his waistcoat and shirt. A hiss escaped him when he pulled the fabric over his shoulders.

A band of dark purple snaked beneath his skin across his abdomen and chest. Gertrude reached out and touched his bare skin, examining the bruises. Nikolai clenched his hands, fisting the fabric of his shirt, and groaned.

"Does it hurt?" She pressed gently.

"Yes. Even more when you prod it." His voice deepened,

husky and rough. It slid over her skin like satin and warmed her like whisky.

Shaking off the lustful thoughts, she focused on the task at hand. "Sit."

Nikolai did as she instructed but kept his trousers on. Judging by her own reaction at his near naked form, this was truly a wise decision on his part. Even though she disapproved of his actions, she brokered no control over her physical reaction to his presence.

With the warm rag, she gently cleaned his face and hair, washing the smears of dirt and blood away. His body tensed beneath her touch. She trailed her fingertips along his scalp and his skin, inspecting for cuts or abrasions. She rinsed the rag and repeated until not a speck of dirt or blood remained.

Using a clean rag, she dabbed the few cuts she found and applied salve she found in the kit. The gash above his eye, however, needed more attention. Fresh blood spilled from the wound as she cleaned it.

"I wish I had some whisky." She muttered under her breath.

"To steady your hand?" Nikolai's soft response startled her.

"No, to clean this needle." She pulled one from the sewing basket along with some strong thread. "This will need stitches to stop the bleeding and save it from scarring."

"Use this." He reached into his trouser pocket and withdrew a flask. "And do not worry about scars. One more will only add to my rakish charm."

"What charm?" Gertrude teased. She poured a bit of the vodka over the needle and threaded it. "And what scars?" Her gaze dropped to his muscular chest. "I see none."

Nikolai leaned forward exposing his back.

Gertrude gasped, her fingers trailed over the overlapping raised scars crisscrossing his strong back disappearing beneath the fabric of his trousers. "Oh, Nikolai."

He leaned back against the chair shielding her gaze from the scars. She pulled her hand away and frowned.

"How did you get these?" she asked, tilting his head back to rest on the chair. Focused on the gash above his eyes, she caught way his jade eyes searched her face before he closed them.

"I made many mistakes as a young man. My punishment left me with scars to carry as a reminder of my transgressions." He winced as she drew the needle through the skin but did not cry out.

"And did the punishment work?" Her soft voice drifted between them.

"Yes." The simple reply came quickly.

"What did it teach you?" She pulled another stitch through.

"Patience." He bore the needle without hesitation.

"Is that all?"

"No." He opened his eyes. Bold and brazen, he replied, "It taught me stealth." He smiled. "I cannot be punished if I am never caught."

"Nikolai." She wished to chastise him but could not. "I doubt this was the intended lesson of the punishment."

"This is true, however, it has served me well over the years."

Gertrude shook the smile from her lips and focused on the last two stitches. "Is this why you prefer the shadows to companionship?" She tied a knot in the last stitch and cut it with a pair of embroidery scissors.

Nikolai's hand wrapped around her wrist. She met his gaze and her heart softened.

"It is true. For years, I preferred to keep to the shadows. For the safety they provide, the anonymity." He pulled her into his lap and the scissors fell to the floor. "But now I choose the light."

Her eyes drifted closed at the soft brush of his fingertips along her jaw. As much as her mind commanded she push him away and demand answers, her heart longed for more of this heat, this passion blossoming between them. She settled against his chest curling into him while trying to keep from pressing against his injuries.

"I never saw the brilliance of the sun until I saw you." He kissed her jaw tenderly. "I never experienced the glory of the starlit sky until I held you in my arms."

"Nikolai...please..." She pulled away from the heat of his

mouth knowing it distracted her reasoning.

"I love you, *liebling*. And nothing, not even the hand of the Almighty himself, will steal my joy. No one shall touch you. You are mine, and I will rain vengeance on anyone who dares to steal you from me."

Chapter Eleven

Nikolai held her tight against his chest, cradling her next to his heart. Her hand rested against his bare skin, and although she did not know it, she branded him with the simple, innocent gesture.

When he murmured the vow against her skin, she stilled, her body trembling almost imperceptibly. He never meant to speak the words aloud, but once they spilled forth, he could no longer deny they were the truth. He loved her, craved her with every fiber of his being. He lived only to protect her.

With her in his arms, the savage beast raging deep in his soul sheathed his claws and settled into the shadows once more. For the last few hours, he indulged the beast's hunger. Anything to uncover the truth. But it lay deeper. Protect her. Knowing their enemies' intentions only fueled his desire to ensure her safety.

Even after hours of interrogation, he found himself lacking the most important information of all. Who was behind this dangerous charade? He found himself no closer to an answer and this infuriated him.

His sides ached. The cuts along his cheek and scalp burned. The seeping gash above his eye throbbed with an unrelenting pulse. Even his lip stung. Her healing touch soothed the pain with every ministration. The beast purred and preened under her tender care. She knew nothing of its past or its power over him.

He trailed his fingers along her neck. "Have I finally rendered you speechless?"

She shivered and nestled closer. "No, I...I feel the same." Gertrude sighed. "But I need answers, Nikolai."

"Pose your questions, *liebling*." He braced himself for the oncoming storm.

"Why are we here?" She tipped her head back to meet his

gaze. "I mean why are we not still in Paris?"

The weight of the past week finally collapsed upon his shoulders. "Someone has threatened the countess."

Her wide eyes shone with understanding. "Have they threatened to kill her? If this is the case, why would you leave her in Paris unguarded?"

"I did not leave her unguarded. I put two of my best men by her side." He shifted her and she settled more comfortably on his lap. "However, I do not believe the countess is their intended target. She is merely the point of contact for negotiation."

"The photograph. It contained a message in Russian." She cocked her head in curiosity. "Will you tell me what it said?"

"*We know the truth. Return, or he dies.*"

Her mouth gaped. "Who dies? What truth?"

Nikolai shook his head. "I do not know. I have no answers."

"The men in the barn?" Her lip trembled at the mention of their existence.

"They told me nothing of importance. Hired thugs sent to subdue me and kill you."

"Kill me?" Gertrude gasped. "Why? I know nothing. I am innocent."

"Exactly. To them, you are worthless. They would rape you and then slit your throat without any hesitation."

Her eyes shone bright with a sheen of tears. "But why?"

"Because they are heartless and cruel. Their only concern is the coin they will make upon my delivery." He stroked his hand along her cheek. "No one will hurt you, *liebling*. Not while I draw breath. This I swear to you."

"The letters." She cleared her throat and began again. "The one from the train I know, but the one from the countess's estate. What did it say?"

"Instructions to come here and wait. Or he will die."

"Who is *he*?" Gertrude scrunched her nose in confusion.

He stifled the urge to kiss her and focused on answering her question. "It could be anyone. The count. Their son. A relative. I do not know. In all possibility, it was merely a ploy to gain compliance. This is why the countess sent me to investigate instead of her coming personally." He scoffed. "I would never allow her to investigate this on her own."

Gertrude nodded thoughtfully then froze. "You said the men came specifically for you?"

"This was the only thing I was able to get from them, even after threatening to remove parts of their anatomy." He snorted. "This always serves as effective motivation to confess."

"Nikolai." Gertrude twisted to face him. The movement brushed her thigh against his groin making him painfully erect, even more so than before. "What if this was their plan all along?"

"To draw me away from the countess in order to bring her harm?" He nodded at her assessment. "I have considered this and taken the proper precautions by leaving her well-guarded. But why me? And why here?"

"Perhaps they wanted to ensure you were properly disposed of before acting on their threat?" She chewed her lip. "I assume you have made many enemies over the course of your life."

Nikolai pondered her assessment. "Of course. A man in my position does not remain there by making friends and coddling enemies."

"Could it be someone from your past who is hellbent on vengeance?" She searched his face. "Someone from your past. Perhaps from the Russian military or even the Okhrana?"

"This is possible. But I have many enemies spread across Europe." He pondered her suggestion. "Yet I have found no connection to any of them upon our journey from Paris to here."

"We must be missing the key to this puzzle." Gertrude tapped her cheek in thought. "What about prior lovers? Could it be you scorned someone in the past and they have decided to take a pound of your flesh in return for their broken heart?"

Nikolai remained impassive, even though he wanted to laugh. Instead, he regarded her seriously for a moment and nodded. "Yes, my former lovers have formed a society of scorned paramours who seek only to torment me for the rest of my life."

She blinked clearly stunned by his jest and then scowled.

"How dare you mock me. I am clearly the only person who wishes to help you solve this mystery. Fine." She twisted from his grip and stood. "I shall leave you to solve your own mysteries and tend your own wounds."

"Come back here." He gripped her wrist and pulled her back into his lap. The force of it knocked the wind from his bruised torso. He pinned her flailing arms in her lap and gripped her jaw with his free hand making her resemble a gasping guppy.

"Jealousy, while it has its place, is quite unnecessary." He released her jaw, brushing his thumb across her lower lip. "I have not had the pleasure of a woman's company in many years. There is no one in my past with such a vendetta. I promise you."

"Oh." She softened against him.

He released her hands and stroked the length of her thigh. "There has only been one woman who has captured my attention. One woman who has haunted me day and night, teasing me with her sweet smile and her enchanting blue eyes."

Gertrude's cheeks bloomed a deep crimson. She gasped as he slid his hand beneath her skirt following the soft fabric until he found hot silken skin. Her thighs fell open and his hand settled heavy between them, cupping her.

"Nikolai." She stuttered and gasped at his insistent touch.

"I curse the fact it took me this long to make myself known." He teased her folds. "But I plan to remedy that."

"Please." She licked her lips, eyes glassy with need.

He rose to his feet, setting her aside for only a moment, and unfastened his trousers. Her gaze followed his hands as he freed his cock.

"Lift your skirts," he commanded.

Blushing so prettily, she obeyed. He hooked his thumbs in her drawers and lowered them to the ground, pulling them free and tossing them aside. Magnificent and proud, she stood with her skirts bunched around her waist and her stockinged legs parted, displaying her beautiful glistening cunt for him alone. His cock bobbed in appreciation.

"You look good enough to eat, *liebling*." He dropped to his knees before her and drew one luscious thigh over his shoulder parting her petals for his perusal.

When he leaned forward and pressed his mouth against her opening, she bucked her hips against his hungry tongue and fisted his hair in her hands.

"Oh, *mein Gott in Himmel.*" A long loud moan poured from deep within her throat when he sucked her flesh.

He teased her, tasting every sweet petal, every silken fold, and then focused on her swollen bud. She thrust her hips against him again, tightening her grip on his hair. Her nails teased the tender skin of his scalp, but Nikolai could not bring himself to care. No. He had her exactly where he wanted her. At his mercy.

Feasting on her, he alternated between soft and hard, slow and fast. Bringing her to the brink of pleasure only to ease away before she reached fulfillment.

"Nikolai," she begged gasping for breath. "Please. I cannot take it much longer."

"You will take what I give you, *liebling.*" He slid his fingers inside her and pressed hard against her walls stroking until her body fluttered around him.

Her grip tightened and a long, deep moan filled the cottage as she came apart beneath his ministrations. Her climax pulsed around his fingers while her cream coated his tongue.

Nikolai savored every delicious drop until she collapsed in a trembling heap beside him on the floor. He gathered her against him, her face buried against his neck.

For several moments they remained thus until her body ceased its convulsions and her breathing slowed to a normal, even rhythm. He stroked her hair and whispered sweet, wicked promises in Russian.

When she finally drew back and met his gaze, he smiled at his handiwork and rose to his feet. Gertrude looked thoroughly fucked, and in a few moments, she would be in every sense of the word. Her curious fingers wrapped around his cock and stroked.

He hissed in a breath. "*Liebling,* once I take you, there is no return. You will be mine until my last breath."

She smiled and kissed him, softly at first, letting it build and grow, evolving into something beyond passion and into desperation. She pushed him down until he lay on the floor gazing up at her glorious face.

Her eyes glinted with mischief and need. When she straddled his hips and pressed his cock to her slick entrance, he groaned.

"You are mine too." She slid him inside, her eyes drifting closed at the welcome invasion.

Her warmth surrounded him, pulling him deep and squeezing him tight. By the stars, it had been too long since he had a woman. He nearly spilled the moment he entered her. His hands settled on her hips and held her still until he regained some control over his baser instincts.

"Hold still, *liebling*, or this will end before it even starts." He inhaled deeply. Once. Twice. Three times, steeling himself against the pull of his climax.

Gertrude leaned down and kissed him softly on the mouth, teasing his lips apart with her tongue. As the kiss deepened, her hips rocked against him. He met every movement with a driving need for more. She rode him hard, her fingertips digging into his shoulders, her teeth scraping along his jaw. Their gasps and moans filled the silent cottage.

She ground her hips against him, her body clenching around his cock pulling them both toward their conclusion. He pressed his fingertips against her swollen folds, and she bucked wildly as her climax ripped his name from her throat.

Her pulsing cunt pushed him over the edge. He tumbled headfirst into pleasure, filling her with his seed, half praying it took root, claiming her without question.

Gertrude collapsed against his chest.

He wrapped his arms around her, holding her close, murmuring endearments in Russian. Waiting for her had been worth every torturous second. He could not regret the past but chose instead to focus on the future.

Whatever came, they would face it together. Nothing would part them from this day forward.

"I love you, *liebling*." He kissed her brow.

She leaned back and met his gaze. Passion stained her cheeks and a sated smile tugged at her lips. "I love you, Nikolai."

He kissed her softly, ignoring the apprehension building in the back of his mind. He could not rest, not until he uncovered the mystery which brought them into the heart of the Alps to an abandoned hunting lodge.

At this moment, there was nothing he could do except remain by Gertrude's side. And this was not a hardship by any means.

Nothing could have prepared her for the rush of emotion currently consuming her for the man beside her. The conflicting pieces overcame her like an avalanche thundering down a mountainside. No matter how much she longed for this, having it come to fruition left her wondering if it were all a fevered dream.

She shivered against him, rubbing her cheek against his bare chest.

"You must eat." Nikolai shifted beneath her and slowly stood. He readjusted his trousers and fastened them around his waist.

Her hungry gaze noted the hard lines of his cock as he tucked it away.

"If you continue to look at me in such a manner, I will toss you over my shoulder and carry you to the bed, where I will keep you indefinitely." His eyes flashed with hunger and humor.

"Perhaps I require that more than food." She smiled even as her stomach growled.

Nikolai laughed. "All in due course, *liebling*." He reached down and lifted her off the floor, setting her down in the chair and covering her lap with a blanket. "Wait here."

The warmth of the blanket could not compete with the inferno of Nikolai. She pulled the blanket up around her throat and watched with fascination as he moved about the room. He placed another kettle over the fire. His muscles flexed beneath the skin of his back as he moved making her body ache with need. He put more wood on the fire and retreated into the pantry on the other side of the room.

Her body hummed with delight from the pleasures they shared. She could not remember sex being as intense and satisfying. Her past experiences were tainted, but discovering this new perspective certainly left her excited to explore the possibilities.

"Here. Eat this." Nikolai reappeared with a small plate filled with a variety of offerings, dried meat, cheese, some bread from the day before, and preserved fruits.

Gertrude accepted the plate and popped one of the fruits in her mouth. The sweet tang lingered and the protesting of her stomach ceased. She ate while her gaze fixed on Nikolai as he prepared two mugs of tea.

She extended the plate toward him when he sat down on the stool beside her chair. He took it and popped a piece of bread in his mouth before setting it aside. They sipped their tea and enjoyed a moment of peaceful silence amidst the growing invisible pressure.

The tea soothed her throat and warmed her through. She cradled the mug in her hand. Even with her belly full and her body sated, she found her mind twisted with questions and fear.

Nikolai reached out and smoothed his finger between her brows and across her forehead. "You wrinkle when you worry."

Her face softened at his words. "You never seem to worry."

He shook his head and scoffed. "*Liebling*, it is my responsibility to ensure you have no need to worry. What thoughts weigh down your mind so heavily?"

"Those men. The letters. Everything." She exhaled deeply trying to expel the unrelenting dread creeping in from the darkness.

"Lorenzo will return shortly with the authorities. They will take care of the men in the barn." He shrugged. "As for the rest, we cannot speculate further. Not until we have more information." A curt nod punctuated his statement. "For now, we wait."

"Yes, you have a point." She sipped the tea and stared into the fire. Questions surfaced unbidden in her mind. While she would much rather take him upstairs and pursue more erotic activities, there were things she wished to know. The lull seemed the perfect opportunity.

"You read my journal." Gertrude studied his strong profile. "How do you know German?"

A smile tugged at the corner of his mouth. "I began teaching myself when I came to work for the countess." His jade eyes flashed. "But I redoubled my efforts when you arrived."

Her heart warmed at the confession. "Why?"

He shrugged a shoulder. "It made me feel closer to you."

The statement seemed so innocuous and yet it endeared him to her even more. "You never speak German." Her face heated. "Except when you call me *liebling*."

"I am afraid my conversational German is quite stunted. I find the pronunciation difficult." He lifted his brow. "However, I read it with ease. Obviously."

"Practice will help you with the pronunciation." She set the empty mug aside and leaned forward. "Would you like me to teach you?"

Nikolai's eyes darkened to the color of a midnight forest. He leveled his gaze with hers. She always viewed him as a predator, but never in her life had she been so keenly aware she was his willing prey.

"I feel we could teach each other a great many things, *liebling*." He kissed her, reigniting the flame of desire smoldering inside her.

Gertrude threw off the blanket and cupped his face between her hands. The stubble along his jaw scraped her palms with a delicious friction. Heat pooled between her thighs. She wanted him with a ferocity that left her shaken. Unbidden, her past rose up and bared its fangs. Her hands fell away and she pulled back, turning toward the fire.

"*Liebling*." Nikolai's fingertips brushed her cheek. She pinched her eyes closed tight in an effort to chase the demons from her mind. "Gertrude." His voice filtered through the haze of the thoughts crowding in upon her. "Gertrude, look at me."

Finally, she inhaled deep and faced him.

Concern etched his brow into an arc over his piercing jade eyes. The stern, guarded Russian wore an almost vulnerable expression.

"What happened?" He smoothed his finger back and forth across the pulse at her throat. "Tell me."

"My husband."

Nikolai stiffened. "You are married?"

Gertrude nodded as the tears began. "I was young and I knew nothing of the world." She wrapped her arms around her torso and blinked away the tears falling freely now. "He took me away from my family. Promised a better life." She shook away the horrible memories. "He lied. I would rather have died of starvation on my parent's farm than live in a fancy house with his abuse."

The murderous glint returned. Nikolai's lips pressed into a thin line as he listened.

"He punished me when I lost our first and only child." She swallowed the knot in her throat. "Because I refused to share a bed with him. Nothing physical, but he locked me away and threatened to have me committed if I did not comply with his demands."

Nikolai wiped the tears from her cheeks but said nothing.

"With the help of several of the servants, I escaped." She paused. "I hid for weeks."

"How did you escape?" He finally spoke.

"During the search, the authorities found a woman in the lake. They assumed it was me from the build and the clothing." She swallowed at the gruesome details. "Her face was damaged beyond recognition. They were convinced it was me, and he was arrested and executed for my murder."

"How long ago?" His rough voice betrayed little emotion.

"Two years before I came to work for the countess." She dabbed her face with the corner of her apron. "My family died in a fire, so there is no one left to search for me. By all accounts, the woman I was is dead. I changed my name and began a new life. Something simple where I would be safe and yet no one would notice me."

"You failed on that count." Nikolai noted with a derisive snort. "I noticed you."

"You notice everyone, Nikolai." She chuckled and sniffed trying to quell what little tears remained.

"I do. But no one has ever captured both my attention and my affection with so little effort." He rearranged them so he sat in the chair and her tucked in his lap. A comforting and familiar position for them both.

She laid her head on his shoulder and he stroked her hair tenderly.

"Why did you not tell me?" he whispered against her forehead.

"Until yesterday, I believed you indifferent, and sometimes even antagonistic, toward me." She kissed his neck. "I did not wish to dwell on the past when the present is much more enticing."

Nikolai hissed in a breath. "If you persist, then I will be forced to take you right here beside the hearth again."

Gertrude wiggled in his lap. "I quite enjoyed it the first time."

"Minx. Do not tease me." He tightened his grip on her waist.

"Why not?" She purred rubbing against his torso. "You tease me every day."

"Do not make me put you over my knee." He growled.

"You have threatened to do so before on multiple occasions." She pulled back and narrowed her gaze searching his face. "I do not think you would actually put me over your knee."

"Is that so?" With his characteristic ease, he shifted her on his lap until she lay sprawling over his knees with her head hanging down and her feet flailing. His hand lay possessively over her backside. His touch burned even through the layers of fabric. "I warned you not to tease me, *liebling*."

He gathered the skirts up and the cool air kissed the still wet folds of her sex. She squirmed at the sensation. He held her steady with his left hand, while his right smoothed over her bare ass.

"Nikolai." She whimpered when his questing fingertips dipped between her thighs. "Please."

He smoothed his rough palm over her right cheek. The touch vanished, and for an instant, she thought freedom lay in her grasp. Without warning, a stinging ache blossomed across her ass as his hand met her flesh. The crack of the impact echoed in the small space.

Gertrude jumped and squirmed against his hold. It did not hurt as much as it startled her, even now, his hot touch soothed the spot.

"Did that hurt?" he asked, his voice husky with desire.

She shook her head and gasped. "No."

"Would you like me to do it again?" He focused his ministrations on the other cheek.

"Yes," she murmured aching for more.

"I cannot hear you." He drew his hand away.

"Yes, please. More." Gertrude cried out trying to twist to see his face.

He held her steady. The crack echoed this time before she registered the bloom of sweet pleasure pain.

A groan of desperation choked her. Unfamiliar sensations and desires rose up from the dusty corners of her mind. She longed to explore them all with Nikolai, only with him. This man who seemed to know her body better than she did.

His fingertips trailed over her sex again, parting her thighs for his inspection. "Oh, *liebling*, I shall never tire of seeing you wet and desperate for me."

In a flurry of skirts and flailing limbs, Gertrude righted herself in his lap and wrapped her arms around his neck. She found his lips and devoured him, tasting the spice of the tea on his tongue and wanting to lose herself to this raging passion forever.

Her hand settled on his cock through his trousers. "I want you inside me." The huskiness of her voice surprised her, but she grinned when she saw the flaring of his nostrils and grit of his jaw.

He rested his hand over hers and stilled both their movement. "Wait." His gaze shifted toward the door. "Listen."

Gertrude froze, listening to the crackle of the logs in the fire and their heavy breaths and the beating of her own heart. The faint thud of footsteps on the wooden boards outside filtered through.

"Lorenzo?" she whispered.

"Wait here." Nikolai stood and set her aside. He stopped by the door and retrieved his gun from his coat pocket.

Gertrude grabbed the poker beside the fire and stood against the wall.

A knock at the door brought them both to attention. Nikolai held his finger to his lips requesting silence and opened the door.

"Please, do not kill me!" a trembling voice cried out at the sight of Nikolai's pistol.

"Coward." Nikolai grabbed the young man and dragged him into the house, tossing him onto the floor. He cocked the pistol and aimed it at the man trembling on the ground. "You led me into an ambush and now you return?" He shook his head. "You must wish for death."

"Please. I had no choice. They threatened my family!" He hid his head beneath his extended arms. "Do not shoot. I have a message."

"Deliver it and get out!" Nikolai growled without lowering the weapon.

"Your presence is demanded." The man scrambled to his feet and bowed his head low, only daring small glimpses at Nikolai. "At the grand hunting lodge."

"Who sends this command?" Nikolai sneered, his aim unwavering.

"The Countess von Breunner." The man opened his fist showing a glinting gold ring with an emerald in the center. "She told me to deliver this along with the message."

Nikolai snatched the ring from his palm and gave it a cursory glance before tucking it in his pocket. "Message received.

Now, get out and do not return!"

The terrified man bolted from the cottage and disappeared into the trees. Nikolai closed the door and leaned against it.

Gertrude stared in complete shock. "Why is the countess here?"

"I do not know." Nikolai inhaled deep and met her steady gaze. "But something is rotten."

Chapter Twelve

Nothing made any sense. The countess set him on this path to uncover the truth, and yet she traveled to the hunting lodge, a place she herself had not visited in years, to speak with him. How in the hell had she even known where to find him?

There were only two people who knew of his location, one stood beside him watching with wide blue eyes and the other sent the letter. It was a trap. It had to be.

He pulled the ring from his pocket and inspected it. Real gold. A genuine emerald glinted in the center. He held it out in his palm.

"I have seen it before among the countess's belongings. Can you verify it belongs to the countess?" Nikolai asked, marking her reaction to the item.

Gertrude plucked the ring from his palm, the brush of her fingertips against his skin sent a wave of need through him. He shoved it aside. The time for answers had arrived. Nothing would distract him from fulfilling his promise to the countess.

She turned it over several times and inspected the inner band before nodding. "Yes, this belongs to her. The count gave it to her several years ago. She does not wear it often."

"Did she have it in Paris?" Suspicion grew inside Nikolai's mind.

Gertrude paused and closed her eyes, her head tilting right and left slightly before her eyes shot open. "Yes. I saw her wearing it at the opera the night before we left Paris."

"At any point, did you notice it missing?"

Confusion marred her lovely brow. "I did not notice one way or another. I typically help the countess store her jewelry after a long evening, but in all the confusion upon receiving the photograph and the hasty return to Vienna, I neglected my duty." She paused. "Do you think someone stole it and is impersonating the countess?"

"I cannot discount it. Why would the countess be here?" He pondered all the possibilities with equal measure. "I relayed nothing of my whereabouts. How would she know exactly where to find me?"

"An astute observation." Gertrude chewed her lip. "The only way to uncover the truth is for us to respond to the summons."

Nikolai shook his head. "You will not be going anywhere."

She propped her hands on her hips. "If you think I will hide in this cottage while you investigate this mystery, you, sir, do not know me at all." She sniffed. "Besides, they know I am with you. What would stop them from coming to the cottage and stealing me away to use as leverage against you?"

He glowered. Her point, while valid, did nothing to ease his conscience. "Very well. I cannot leave you here." Taking her by the shoulders, he drew her close and held her gaze. "You will listen to my instructions. If I give you an order, you obey it."

"I believe you enjoy giving me orders."

"I only wish to keep us both alive." He gritted his teeth. "Do you understand my instructions?"

"Yes." She softened against him and wrapped her arms around his waist. "I trust you, Nikolai."

This beautiful woman held his heart in her hands. If he lost her, he would rain fire and brimstone down upon those who dared to steal her away. Keeping her beside him would be the only way to ensure her safety.

He pressed a kiss to the crown of her head. "Remember, *liebling*, whatever happens, you belong to me. We are bound in this life and the next."

After a few moments, Nikolai reluctantly pulled from her embrace. He gestured to her warm clothes. "You have a pocket in this skirt?"

She rearranged the folds to reveal a small slit along her hip. "Yes. Why?"

Nikolai reached into his coat and pulled out the small pistol he used earlier. "Do you know how to use this?"

Gertrude nodded and took the weapon.

"Good. Do not take it out unless you intend to use it." He leveled his gaze with hers. "I would never ask you to take a life, but if you must in order to save yourself, then do not hesitate."

"I understand." She swallowed hard and gave a shaky nod.

"Very well. Put on your drawers and winter outer garments. Hurry." Nikolai considered wearing his bloody, torn clothing, but instead he donned a fresh shirt and a warm sweater Lorenzo lent from his own wardrobe.

Once they were suitably dressed and armed, Nikolai led the way into the cold afternoon. They slogged through the knee-high snow. Gertrude followed behind, stepping in his footprints, as he broke the path to give her easier passage. It also betrayed only one set of prints should anyone happen upon them.

No sound emanated from the barn as they passed. The men inside could be dead for all he knew or cared. *Let them rot.*

Their heavy breaths echoed in the eerie stillness of the fresh, snow-covered forest. They ducked beneath branches and wove along the path he traveled upon their arrival at the cottage. Nothing seemed disturbed, and yet such peace brought with it a thread of unease.

When they reached the clearing beside the hunting lodge manor house, Nikolai stopped and pressed his fingers to his lips requesting silence.

Gertrude nodded with understanding and followed as he wove around the tree line to the front of the building.

The house looked shuttered as before, but he noticed several windows lay uncovered. Soft light danced inside the windows revealing its occupation. He tightened his grip on the pistol in his pocket and approached the steps leading to the front door.

"Stay close," he whispered over his shoulder.

Gertrude crept closer. He could almost feel the warmth of her against his back as they ascended the stairs.

The door swung open when he reached for the handle. A short, blond man with a pistol aimed straight at Nikolai's heart stood in the warm lodge.

"Welcome, Mr. Voronia. You are late." His strong accent bore the distinct traces of Russian heritage.

Nikolai slowly withdrew his hand from his pocket and raised both into the air.

"I see you brought a guest." The man stepped aside. "Please, come in."

They stepped inside the house, and Nikolai shielded Gertrude from the man's view.

"Check them both for weapons." The blond man instructed when two men appeared from the shadows.

Nikolai grit his teeth at the brusque handling of his person. The man searched his pockets, retrieving his gun without much effort. His gaze however remained on the man attempting to search Gertrude.

She bundled herself deeper into her cloak and pulled away from the intrusion.

"Do not touch her," Nikolai snapped when the brute wrapped his hand around her wrist and twisted her arm.

The man sneered at him before resuming his search. He patted the pockets of her cloak and slid his hands along her bodice. Gertrude whimpered and cringed against the assault.

"Touch her again, and I will break every bone in your body and leave you to the wolves." Nikolai's threat hung in the air like a dense fog.

With a scoff, the man dropped his hands from her person and stepped away. The two henchmen stepped back flanking the blond gunman who now held two guns trained on both of them.

"This way." The man jerked the pistol barrels toward a large arched doorway.

Nikolai took Gertrude's hand and together they led the way into the indicated room. He squeezed her trembling hand hoping to give her comfort in his presence.

Inside, the men fanned out to the sides, keeping them focused on the center of the room. The rich, vibrant blue walls decorated with stag heads and antlers. A large bearskin rug lay in the center of the floor in front of the hearth. Two leather wingback chairs flanked the hearth where a fire blazed. Mahogany tables stood sentry beside them, while a large sofa sat opposite the hearth with a suede leather skin draped across it and accented with sheepskin blankets.

Nikolai searched the shadows near the large curtained windows and noted the two doors leading to rooms beyond. He saw only three of them, but there were more lurking in the shadows. He would stake his life on it.

"Where is our host?" Nikolai asked the question as one would inquire after the weather. He tempered his emotion into submission focusing only on the task of locating the countess.

The door to the right of the hearth opened.

Gertrude's hand tightened around his, and she gasped. "Your Grace."

The countess stepped into the room wearing a red velvet gown trimmed with ermine fur. Her uneven steps and the tight press of her mouth showcased her displeasure much more effectively than words. Her silver hair lay unbound over her shoulders and her typically bright eyes bore the marks of exhaustion. Fury lay in their depths.

Nikolai recognized it instantly. She had been brought here against her will. He failed her.

At the imperceptible shake of her head, Nikolai bit back the question forming on his tongue. Instead, he reached into his pocket and withdrew the ring the innkeeper's son delivered.

"I believe this belongs to you." He extended it with a bow.

Without a word, she retrieved it. Her touch lingering for a moment longer than necessary as if to convey a sense of comfort or relay an unspoken message.

"Your Grace..." Nikolai began, unable to bear the shame of his failure.

"Silence!" Her command echoed through the room. Nikolai snapped his mouth closed and stood at reverent attention.

How could this be? Had he been so blind as to abandon his sworn duty to protect the countess? The photograph. The letters. They were nothing but a game to lead him astray, to keep him distracted. *Fool.* He cursed himself repeatedly.

Tears formed in the countess's eyes. Her lip trembled even as she tipped her chin up in a show of strength.

"I gave you a simple task, Nikolai." Her gaze drifted to his hand which lay clasped with Gertrude's. Her expression softened almost imperceptibly.

"Yes, Your Grace." He remained steadfast.

"I trusted you with my life and the lives of my children." She took a half step closer, the ring twisting between her fingers.

"I apologize for my inadequacies." He met her gaze steadily. "I failed you."

"No, Nikolai." She replied softly. "It is I who have failed you."

With great difficulty, her words permeated his shame. "I do not understand."

"I believe, what the countess is trying to tell you in her own, convoluted way, is she is the reason for the situation in which you find yourself." The disembodied voice filtered through the doorway. The cultured French accent familiar and yet cold and calculated.

The soft-spoken doctor from their journey on the Alpine Express entered the room, his dark eyes glinting behind the glass of his spectacles.

"Dr. Archer?" Surprise reflected in Nikolai's voice.

"So confident, so astute, and yet it seemed my act was enough to fool even the great Nikolai Voronia." He tucked his hands into his tweed trouser pockets and rocked back on his heels. "I have been watching you for quite some time. But it was only when I recently obtained a new bit of information, my suspicions were solidified."

The countess watched him carefully, the ring twisting faster between her fingers. Nikolai remained focused on the diminutive, innocuous doctor.

"What suspicions?" Nikolai demanded. "And why the elaborate game?" He released Gertrude's hand and stepped closer sizing up his miniscule opponent.

The sound of multiple guns cocking brought him up short. He flexed his hands.

Dr. Archer reached into his breast pocket and withdrew a letter. He carefully unfolded it and held it out between two fingers. "Read it."

Nikolai snatched it from his hand and scanned the contents. "I cannot read this. It is in French."

"I can." Gertrude stepped forward and took the letter. Her eyes widened with every word.

The doctor's grin stretched.

"What in the devil does it say?" Nikolai grew impatient with the growing tension.

Gertrude licked her lips and met his gaze. "According to classified sources close to the Russian royal family, you are the son of Czar Alexander II. His bastard son."

Nikolai stumbled back. His vision blurred as his mind raced. "It cannot be." He shook his head and tore the paper from her grip. "Where is your proof?"

"The proof is in the mirror, Nikolai. You bear a striking resemblance to the late czar." The countess reached for him only to drop her hand at the last moment when he stepped away.

Everything he believed shattered before him. He knew he was born out of wedlock, but a royal bastard? This changed things dramatically.

Tension hung thick in the air. Gertrude choked back the questions forming on the tip of her tongue. This was not her battle. Instead, she bolstered her strength and remained silent beside Nikolai.

A royal bastard. The revelation, as absurd as it sounded, struck a chord of truth somewhere in the depths of her soul. She could not confirm the claim, but judging from the countess's haunted green eyes and sallow pallor, the affirmation solidified.

Nikolai stood tall and still as a statue, his face seemingly carved from stone. His gaze flickered between the doctor and the countess. There was little indication of emotion upon his features, hidden by the stoic mask of indifference he utilized so frequently in public. She knew, better than most, his mind was working quickly to ascertain proof of this statement presented as fact.

Her attention drifted to the men surrounding them at different points around the room. One leaned against the fireplace. Two near the far door where they entered earlier. Another pair lounged in the shadows beyond the doctor. All of them armed in some form or fashion, ready for a single order. Gertrude suppressed a shiver.

"Your mother served as a maid in the Winter palace, did she not?" Dr. Archer's sardonic smile churned her stomach.

Nikolai said nothing in response.

"When it was discovered she was unwed and pregnant, she was dismissed from her position." He paused as if gauging the effect of his words on Nikolai. "She took refuge with the local congregate of nuns, where you were born. They aided her in securing another position in the kitchens of a large estate outside St. Petersburg."

"I have never hidden the fact I was born a bastard or poor." The tone of his voice rumbled through the room carrying an undercurrent of thinly veiled contempt.

"Yes, but you rarely share anything about your past. In fact, many of your former acquaintances, some of whom you spent many years serving with, seem to have no information as to your history whatsoever." The doctor cocked his head. "How peculiar."

"Get to the point," Nikolai growled.

The doctor tutted and gestured to the leader of his pack of thugs who maintained his pistol's aim on them. "One should never rush a good tale."

Even the subtle threat did nothing to shake Nikolai's steel façade.

The countess, much like Nikolai, remained steadfast and stoic. Her pale skin and the dark patches beneath her eyes made her look gaunt. The image much at odds with the vivacious, eccentric woman she served for the last five years. She met Gertrude's gaze and pressed her lips into a thin line. Regret shone across her features. Regret and pain.

"Now, where was I?" The doctor tapped his chin thoughtfully and readjusted his glasses. "Yes, your military career. It seemed a given choice of vocation considering your less-than-ideal upbringing, and yet you thrived, rising in the ranks and earning the recognition of a loyal soldier." He smirked. "Do you remember the day your father died?"

Nikolai's jaw flexed as if bracing himself against the memory.

"Of course, you do. You remember every vivid detail of that day. Your curse and your blessing, that memory of yours." He chuckled. "Yes, your comrades spoke of your gift for committing things to memory in crystalline detail." The doctor waved a hand when Nikolai did not respond. "Your actions earned you high accolades and brought you one step closer to the truth of your birth, even if you did not realize it at the time."

"I knew nothing of my father." Nikolai held the doctor's gaze.

"But someone must have." He grinned again, enjoying the power he held over them. "Someone recognized you as an almost perfect replica of the young czar."

"None of this matters. The czar is dead. His son is dead. And his grandson sits on the throne." Nikolai remained impassive, but Gertrude sensed the turmoil twisting inside him. "Your tale has nothing to do with me."

"Oh, but it has everything to do with you, Mr. Voronia." The doctor leaned against the chair. "Someone figured out your secret. Someone with close ties to the royal family and a deep sense of loyalty." His gaze shifted to the countess.

Gertrude gasped as the implication fell into place connecting all the pieces of the larger picture.

"Tell him." The doctor demanded the countess. "Now."

The countess flinched but rolled her shoulders and lifted her chin, elevating her gaze with dignity. She slid the ring on her finger and sighed.

"There were rumors throughout the city the ghost of my uncle roamed the shadows, searching for traitors and seeking revenge." She scoffed. "I ignored them until you arrived on my doorstep carrying my son over your shoulder." Tears glinted in her eyes. She dashed them away with the back of her hand and cleared her throat.

"The moment I saw you, I knew you were his son." She shook her head. "There was not a doubt in my mind. But I could not allow you to leave, not until I could research further." Her voice caught with emotion. "I only wanted to protect you, Nikolai." The tears fell freely this time.

Gertrude saw the stony façade crack and his body soften at the impact of her words. Nikolai flexed his hands repeatedly before he spoke.

"Why did you not tell me the truth?" he asked, his voice deceptively composed.

"Until two weeks ago, I had no concrete evidence to support my suspicions." The countess sniffed and glared at the doctor. "Unfortunately, I also discovered I was not the only person who had been searching for this information."

"Yes, how fortuitous we happened upon the same resource." The doctor mused with a chuckle. "I admit, I was searching for a ghost, a rumor. I had no idea the man in question stood within my grasp."

"You sent the photograph!" Gertrude said aloud, regretting the spontaneous reaction almost instantly. She pursed her lips and hung her head.

"Bravo." He clapped his hands in a mock celebration of her revelation. "I knew the countess would never leave Paris so quickly after having just arrived. But if someone she loved were threatened...I realized she may be persuaded to abandon her beloved hound."

"The photograph." Nikolai pinched his eyes closed. "The royal family."

"Your cousins and siblings, to be more precise." The doctor preened at his own genius. "My way of informing the countess she was not alone in her knowledge."

Nikolai nodded. "You followed us onto the train, ensuring our arrival in Vienna."

The doctor slowly nodded, his eyes bright behind the spectacles.

"You searched my compartment."

Gertrude watched the volley with rapt attention. The details of the plot unraveled before her eyes.

"How astute of you, Mr. Voronia. It took you long enough to figure it out." Dr. Archer paced the floor like a teacher lecturing a student. "Imagine my delight when I realized the good major was also aboard the Alpine Express. He certainly kept you distracted."

"Son of a bitch," Nikolai muttered. "You played us against each other in order to remain inconspicuous."

"It worked better than I ever could have hoped." The doctor laughed. "Seeing you two engaged in such open hostility left me better able to gather as much information as I could without gaining suspicion." He tisked. "Really. I am quite disappointed in you after hearing about the legendary Okhrana soldier."

Gertrude felt the energy of the gathering storm inside Nikolai. She reached down and took his hand. He drew her against him, their hands hidden in the folds of her skirt.

"Why do you care about who I am?" Nikolai asked, his fingers sliding along her skirt.

It took her a moment to realize he was searching for her pocket. She slowly guided him to the break in the fabric where the gun lay heavy against her hip. Her nervous gaze darted to each of the armed men before centering on the doctor.

"I have been paid, quite handsomely, to uncover those with any claim to the throne." He nodded to two of the men who disappeared out the side door. "My employer will be meeting me in Salzburg once I have concluded this little reunion and successfully eliminated the three of you."

"Your employer must be paying you handsomely to murder the countess." Nikolai's hand settled over the pistol.

"A matter I will kindly address upon our meeting." The doctor shifted his weight and adjusted his glasses. "My price has doubled, although I see no objection since the man in question has grotesquely deep pockets and no moral scruples."

"Ah, the powerful elite." Nikolai scoffed. "That narrows it down."

"You have no idea how powerful these men are, Mr. Voronia." He licked his lips. "Crossing them would be most imprudent."

"As is crossing me." Nikolai drew the pistol and rounded on the man beside the hearth. He fired and the man dropped gripping his wounded shoulder.

Gertrude dove toward the countess, pulling her to the ground. She covered her as Nikolai spun and fired twice more. All motion in the room slowed creating a vortex of time. She watched in horror as one of the men charged Nikolai.

"No!" She jumped up to intercede, only to be snatched by the back of her dress and pulled roughly against a warm body.

"Shut up!" His grip tightened. "One false move and I put a bullet in her skull."

Gertrude whimpered at the press of a pistol barrel against her temple.

Nikolai slowly rose from the floor where one of the henchmen lay writhing at his feet. The gash above his eye bled profusely, the stiches torn open leaving it ragged. Smears of fresh blood and rivulets painted his skin. A vengeful angel come to destroy the wicked.

The doctor tightened his grip on Gertrude. "I am warning you. On your knees."

Without blinking, Nikolai dropped to his knees.

Dr. Archer leveled the gun at him.

Gertrude threw her weight back against him, driving her elbow into his side. When she slipped from his grasp, his hand tangled around the braids crowning her head drawing her up short. Pain ripped through her scalp.

"Bitch!" He brought the gun down hard.

A stabbing, blinding agony shot through the back of her skull. Gertrude screamed, and the world collapsed into darkness.

CHAPTER THIRTEEN

Blood coursed hot and thick through his veins. Every sense on alert, Nikolai took measure of his opponents long before the first strike. Dropping the goons proved easier than he anticipated, and those who were out of his reach ran like terrified rabbits. He spun around to see his worst fear become reality and it struck him like a saber through heart.

Gertrude crumpled to the ground, limp and lifeless. Her scream echoed in Nikolai's ears, releasing the unfettered rage he restrained for her safety. Unbridled fury consumed him. He leapt to his feet and charged forward.

The doctor turned the pistol back to Nikolai, his eyes widening at the incoming assault. He pulled the trigger. The flash of the powder and the deafening crack of the shot should have deterred his assault. The horrific agony of the bullet shredding his flesh made him stumble. But nothing could stop him from killing the man responsible for the suffering he in which he found himself drowning.

Nikolai wrapped his arms around the doctor's waist, the force of the impact knocked them both to the ground. The gun skittered across the floor to the opposite side of the room. Rising up, Nikolai unleashed the monster inside. His fists dealt blow after blow until the doctor whimpered unable to block the blows with his arms across his face.

Rage and betrayal gathered like a maelstrom in the depths of his withered soul. Warm blood blurred his vision and exhaustion tore his body apart.

"Nikolai!" The countess's command severed the haze of bloodlust.

He pulled away from the unconscious doctor and collapsed against the floor. His breath came in harsh puffs. Wiping a sleeve across his face, Nikolai cleared his vision and found the countess standing over him with the pistol in her delicate hands. Her gaze drifted to a spot behind him.

"*Liebling.*" Against the protest of his aching body, Nikolai dragged himself to her side. She lay like a rag doll tossed carelessly on the thick rug. Her lashes rested against her pale cheek. Was she dead? He pressed his hand against her chest. A soft pulse responded to his questing touch.

"Is she alive?" the countess asked, coming alongside him.

"Yes. But she will need a physician." Nikolai glared at Dr. Archer who lay a few feet away.

"Bring her to one of the rooms. I shall deal with these fiends and then offer my aid."

Nikolai raised a brow in question but refrained from asking how she would exactly deal with the men who had kidnapped and nearly killed them. Instead, he nodded and gently gathered Gertrude in his arms. Her weight settled comfortably against him, and although his body screamed in protest, he carried her into the hallway and up the stairs.

The first door opened with some help from his booted foot. The furniture lay covered with sheets. He frowned at the thin layer of dust upon them. He carefully placed her upon the bed and rearranged the counterpane. Shifting her into a more comfortable position, he swore at the smear of blood beneath her head on the linens.

Nikolai took his time removing her outer garments and boots. He spoke in soft soothing tones, murmuring in both Russian and English.

Shouts echoed outside the room through the cavernous hallways. The countess! He darted from the room to find a regimen of soldiers gathering on the stairs. Relief flooded him even as they trained their weapons on him.

"Hold your fire. He is mine." The countess's sharp command rang through the entryway. "The men you want are in here. And someone fetch the doctor in the village. Now!"

Nikolai smiled at the ease with which the countess took control of the unorthodox situation. She truly possessed a warrior's spirit. They had much to discuss, but first, he needed to focus on Gertrude.

"You." He pointed to two of the soldiers. "Fetch me some wood and water."

The men nodded and promptly retreated out into the cold.

Nikolai gestured to the other men. "Search the rest of the house. Ensure there are no other men lurking in the shadows."

Once he returned to Gertrude's side, confidence infused him. With everything in hand, he could focus on her. He slid her cold hand between his.

"*Liebling*, return to me." He kissed her pallid cheek and recoiled at the smear of blood it left behind.

He glanced at the far wall behind him where a small mirror hung and cringed at his reflection. His hair struck out at odd angles, the gash above his eye had burst open during the fight and bled profusely leaving a trail of bright red smeared across his face. A warrior drenched in the blood of his enemies. He scoffed. More like his own.

After wiping a great deal of the blood from his face, he returned to Gertrude's side. She remained still, her chest barely rising with every breath.

The two soldiers burst into the room, as well as the countess. She barked instructions, having them build a fire and put a kettle of water on. Her gaze softened when she spotted him.

"My faithful protector." She brushed her fingers along his cheek. "You should sit down before you collapse."

As if summoned from the air, a chair appeared. The countess's silent instructions to the soldiers proved how efficient and well-respected she truly was. She motioned to the chair and arched a brow in challenge.

The rush of battle began to fade into an overwhelming exhaustion. Nikolai collapsed onto it, groaning at the ache sinking into his very bones. His head pounded and every extremity felt as though it weighed a ton.

"Rest your eyes. I will tend to Gertrude."

Even though his mind fought for consciousness, the

instructions released the remaining tension in his body. The room faded into swirling colors and then fell completely into the darkness.

Dreams came swiftly. Lovely scenes with Gertrude wrapped in his embrace. Her golden hair spread over silken sheets. Her succulent mouth parted on a gasping moan. His mouth on her soft skin trailing kisses and laying claim.

The dream shifted like sand in an hourglass turning dark and covering the world in mist. Faceless men prowled closer. Gertrude's scream piercing the darkness somewhere beyond his reach. He ran, searching and crying out in earnest. Terror gripped his heart.

A throne covered in blood. The Romanov family crest hung above it, ripped in half, smoldering in ashes. Nikolai ran until the sea surrounded him. He called for her, but the water choked him.

His eyes flew open. A damp compress lay across his head. The countess's smiled down at him.

Nikolai shifted. He lay in a bed. Even though his body screamed at the motion, he sat up. "Where is she?"

Sweat clung to his skin. He pulled at the sheet, covering his chest. Conscious of his undressed state, he glanced at the countess who stood patiently beside the bed.

"Gertrude is still asleep. The doctor has assessed her and dressed the wound on her head." The countess's words eased the fear gripping his heart. She offered a mug of steaming liquid. "Drink."

He sipped the concoction hoping for something stronger than tea. The bitter aftertaste made him shiver. "What the hell is that?"

"A tea designed to help you heal." She nodded to the mug in his hands. "Finish it."

Nikolai swore. "I must see her." He moved to climb from the bed, but the countess shook her head.

"You will remain in bed until the doctor returns tomorrow." She narrowed her gaze and pinned him with the regal stare. "You need rest. If you tear open those stitches, I will let you bleed to death."

A throbbing ache permeated his shoulder. He pressed his hand to the wound and hissed in a breath. Damn it. He completely forgot he had taken a bullet.

The countess propped up the pillows at the head of the bed. "Sit back. Rest. Do not argue with me." She raised a finger when he opened his mouth.

He snapped it closed and leaned back against the pillows, eyeing her with distaste.

"I understand your anger." The countess dabbed a fresh cloth against his brow being careful of the gash over his right eye.

Avoiding her gaze, Nikolai focused on the fire flickering in the hearth on the other side of the room. He cradled the tea in his hands and refrained from speaking, knowing it would only sound bitter and callous.

"It was wrong of me to keep my suspicions to myself for so many years." Regret laced her words. "I should have been honest with you from the beginning. Especially after you risked your own life to save my son's. For that, I will always be in your debt."

"You owe me nothing." Nikolai struggled with the internal battle raging against his better judgment.

"You know, as well as I, this is untrue. My family owes you a debt of gratitude that cannot be repaid." She dropped her gaze and fidgeted with the blanket, pulling it up over his chest. "You deserved to know the truth of your past. I was wrong to keep it from you."

Nikolai exhaled deeply and closed his eyes. "I should have known something was amiss. The looks I garnered. The questions I faced. But never once did I suspect something of this magnitude." He shook his head. "I am not noble, even though my blood may be."

The countess nodded. "You must have many questions."

Nikolai met her gaze. "I have only one."

"Ask, Nikolai. And I will do my best to answer it."

"When you received the photograph, did you not suspect to whom they referred in their threat?" He studied her stern expression.

She hung her head, shielding her eyes. "The photograph depicted every direct heir of the Romanov lineage." Tears streaked down her face. "Even my son at a young age."

"But did you believe they meant him?"

Her head shook repeatedly. "No. There was a mystery to it at first, but it was not until you left on the Alpine Express, I realized what the message meant. By then it was too late." Those tear laden eyes met his. "I had no way to contact you without raising their suspicions."

Nikolai nodded uneasy but satisfied with her honesty. "It is not like I have tried to hide my presence. How has it taken this long for them to discover my location?"

The countess swore under her breath. "I blame my son. He returned to Moscow a few weeks ago and partook in some, shall we call it, unsavory activities." Her scowl marred the delicate skin of her face. "He got drunk and spoke of the family, of our past. Of his past. Well, they were able to discern the connection between the Okhrana operative and the man who saved his life."

"I see." Nikolai pondered this information wondering if he should have let the blackguard rot in a hell of his own device. Then he remembered Gertrude. If he had not helped the countess's son, then he never would have met the love of his life.

"You have gone above and beyond to protect me and my family, what can I offer in return?"

Nikolai reached out and tipped her chin up until their eyes locked. "Release me."

"What?" The countess dashed the tears from her eyes.

"The debt has been paid. Once I have recovered, I will leave and darken your door no longer." He closed his eyes and leaned back against the pillows.

"If this is your wish, it shall be done." He heard the countess slowly retreat from the room and close the door behind her. Then he sank into a fitful slumber and dreamed of the day when he and Gertrude could escape this house and its lies forever.

Gertrude blinked against the light coming in through the curtains. Her body lay heavy against a plush cloud of fabric. What happened? She blinked rapidly as the memories filtered through a haze of confusion. Nikolai. The countess. Fear shot through her and a scream lodged in her throat.

"Shhh, my dear. You are safe." The countess appeared by her side. Dark spots beneath her eyes and a weary smile aged her beyond her fifty-five years.

"Your Grace." Gertrude's voice cracked. "You are alive." Relief flooded her banishing the fear which gripped her only moments before. "Nikolai?"

The countess nodded. "He is recovering in the next room." A maternal smile tugged at her lips. "I will fetch him, but you must drink some tea first." She tugged the bell pull next to the bed and a servant arrived immediately. Once she ordered tea and some broth, the servant retreated leaving them alone once more.

She lifted her arm with conscious effort and rubbed her eyes with the back of her hand. Pain radiated through the back of her head, along her spine, and into her hips. She groaned and shifted wanting to alleviate the ache in her bones.

With the countess's help, she sat up, propped against a mountain of pillows. Her fingers brushed over the bandage wrapped around her head.

"We can remove it now." The countess sat beside her and carefully unwound the bandage.

"What happened?" Gertrude's curiosity outweighed any remaining modesty or propriety.

"Dr. Archer struck you." She set aside the bandages and picked up a brush, setting to the task of dressing her hair. "You have been unconscious for some time."

The countess's gentle touch soothed her as she unbound and untangled her snarled hair. "How long?"

"It has been nearly five days."

Gertrude gasped. "What happened...after I..." She trailed

off unable to even formulate the words surrounding the incident.

"Nikolai saved you." The countess shook her head with a sad smile. "He saved both of us." Her eyes blazed blue with fervor.

"Is it true? Nikolai's past...his birth?" Gertrude brushed off the discomfort of asking such a question. The truth had been revealed, but she wished to hear the words from someone who cared for Nikolai and welcomed him into her family.

"Yes, it is true." The countess paused when the door opened and a maid entered carrying a silver tray laden with tea and a steaming bowl of mutton broth. She dismissed the servant and regarded Gertrude for a moment before setting aside the brush.

"One night many years ago, Nikolai appeared on my doorstep and everything I believed of the world changed in a single moment." The countess poured two cups of tea with grace and ease. Her voice betrayed not a tremor as she told her tale. "He pushed past the servants with my inebriated son tossed over his shoulder like a sack of potatoes. I should have thanked him and sent him on his way, but when he stepped into the light, I noticed the blood dripping from my son's fingertips trailing across the parquet floor."

She offered the cup and saucer. "Careful, my dear. You are still quite weak."

Gertrude accepted it with thanks, blowing across the top of the cup before taking a tentative sip. She waited with impatience for the countess to continue her story. A curious need to know the details of Nikolai's past burned through her.

"Without waiting for an explanation, I sent the footman for the physician and led the mysterious savior carrying my son to the nearest bed chamber." She sipped her tea and sighed; her gaze unfocused as she lost herself in the memory. "It wasn't until the physician arrived and set to tending the bullet hole in my son's arm that I turned my attention to his savior. I demanded to know what happened."

The countess's voice softened. "He removed his hood and scarf, revealing his face. His eyes nearly black in the shadows, the strong line of his jaw and the firm set of his mouth. Handsome and foreboding, but he looked familiar. As I questioned him, the pieces fell into place."

"He found my son gambling in a den near the palace. There was an altercation between the players. My son, who had been caught cheating, was shot." She inhaled deeply. "I am grateful Nikolai stepped in when he did, otherwise my son would have been left for dead."

Gertrude clung to the porcelain tighter afraid to interrupt the countess.

"Nikolai revealed his position with the Okhrana, which explained his knowledge of our family and his presence in such a place. However, his decision to intervene left him vulnerable to retaliation. Revealing his identity merely sealed his fate." The countess took another drink and set the cup aside.

"Did you suspect his relationship to the Romanov family at this point?" The question spilled from her lips with breathless anticipation.

The countess shook her head. "It was not until the next morning, when I saw him in the light of day, I fully recognized the similarities. I located an old portrait of my uncle, the czar, from his younger days. There was no denying his legitimacy." She pressed her lips together. "But I could not allow him to remain in Russia. Not after the incident with my son."

"You offered the position as your personal guard." Gertrude filled in the details with what she already knew.

"We agreed it would be a mutual arrangement. He could leave my employ at any time, should he choose to do so. I compensated him handsomely to remain by my side."

"Was this for your safety or his?" Gertrude asked before considering the implications of her words.

The countess's lip curled in amusement. "I will admit, at the time, my intentions were purely selfish. But as the years passed, I feared someone would make the connection as I had." She took the tea from Gertrude's hand and set it aside, replacing it with the bowl of soup.

Gertrude lifted the bowl to her lips and drank. The warm

broth settled in her stomach easing the hunger and warming her throughout.

"I sent instructions to some of the best, and most discreet, investigators throughout Europe, ones I knew who would have no allegiance to a monarchy or any other political group." She folded her hands in her lap and continued her tale. "They were able to locate his mother's relatives, who revealed the truth of his conception and subsequent banishment."

"In Paris, I received notice to meet with my contact who possessed the documentation which gave verification to Nikolai's birth."

"What does that mean?" Gertrude asked between sips.

"Nikolai may not be in line for the throne, however he is part of the Romanov family. This information would cast a bleak shadow over the czar's position. Alexander II was known for his stance in alleviating the tensions between the serfs and the nobility through reform. In the end, this only elevated tensions among the divided classes. If it came to light he fathered a child with a servant, it would intensify the chaos now churning throughout Russia." She hung her head. "I fear Russia, if not all of Europe, will be entering a difficult period if this unrest persists as it has for decades. I did not wish for Nikolai to be the proverbial match that sets off this powder keg."

"Do you have such little faith in humanity?" Nikolai's deep voice echoed from the doorway.

Gertrude and the countess turned at the intrusion. Her heart jumped at the sight of him alive. She set the bowl of broth aside.

"Nikolai, please, join us." Gracefully, the countess rose to her feet maintaining her composure. A telltale blush tinged her cheeks, but she remained collected when he entered the room.

A lock of his hair lay across the bandage on his temple. He brushed it away stifling a groan at the limited mobility of his bandaged left arm. The exhaustion seemed to have lifted only to be replaced with concern.

"How much did you hear?" The countess inclined her head.

"Everything." He sat on the edge of the bed and reached

for Gertrude's hand. His fingers interlaced with hers, and he smiled. The action softened the harsh lines of his face and brightened his eyes. "I was worried you would never wake." His voice cracked. "I thought I lost you."

Gertrude cupped his cheek in her hand as tears filled her eyes. Emotion choked her. When she finally found her voice, she whispered, *"Mein Herz."*

A delicate cough reminded her they were not alone. Gertrude stole a glance at the countess, who watched them, her eyes damp with unshed tears.

"I am glad something positive came from this horrific disaster." The countess beamed. "It took both of you long enough. I feared I would be forced to drastic measures in order to bring you together."

Nikolai snorted. "How could you have possibly known..."

"Darling. You underestimate me yet again. I have spent the last five years watching the two of you tempt each other, dancing around the edges of flirtation. There were times I worried you were more concerned with Gertrude's well-being than my own should something catastrophic happen." She shrugged an elegant shoulder in dismissal, but Gertrude recognized the countess's veiled humor and laughed.

"And you, my dear. I happen to know more of your secrets than even you realize." She tapped her lips as she pondered. "I researched your employment references a bit more and found some interesting details about your history. According to your previous employer, while you were a dedicated servant, they took quite a chance on taking you into their home. Since they found you wandering in the forest, bedraggled and hungry."

Fear gripped Gertrude's heart and squeezed. Nikolai's fingers smoothed over her hand in a soothing motion. She dropped her gaze at the countess's assertion. "Why did you not turn me out?"

"Why would I shun my best companion?" the countess asked. "You have never given me cause to doubt you. Besides, I know a lost soul in need of shelter when I see one." Her gaze shifted to Nikolai briefly.

"I thank you for your kindness." A sense of impending finality settled within Gertrude's soul, and with Nikolai beside her, the uncertainty of the future did not overwhelm her as it once would have.

"I shall take my leave and allow you both some time to discuss what comes next." With a pointed look, the countess left them.

Nikolai settled closer to her on the bed and drew her against his chest. She burrowed into his warmth, ignoring the aching protests of her injuries.

"What happened?" Her hand brushed his bandaged shoulder.

"Bullet." Nikolai kissed her head.

Gertrude pulled back to search his face. "What do you mean, bullet? Who shot you?"

"The double crossing doctor. He knocked you unconscious and then shot me when I lunged for him." Nikolai recited this in the same manner someone would discuss the weather.

She jabbed her elbow into his ribs. "Why would you do something so ridiculous? He could have killed you."

"He failed." A smirk tugged his lips. She hated how one simple action made her heart race.

"I could have lost you forever." The thought left her untethered in a sea of despair. She brushed her fingertips along his stubbled jaw needing the contact to reassure herself he was truly there. Alive and completely hers.

"It is over. He has been dealt with." He wrapped his hand around her wrist and brought it to his lips. Her body warmed at the intimate press of his mouth against her skin.

"You killed him." The idea left her relieved.

"No. But he will never again be a free man." He smirked. "Nor will his face heal properly. I can guarantee that."

Gertrude pushed the grotesque thoughts from her mind. "What happens next?"

"I have already spoken with the authorities and given my account of the events. They have agreed to keep the details of the case a secret, per the request of the countess." Nikolai sighed.

"But we cannot return to Vienna."

"We?" Happiness bloomed inside her heart.

"Yes, *liebling*, where I go, you go, remember?" Nikolai kissed her softly.

She leaned into him savoring the warm, spicy scent of him and the need unfurling inside her.

"If you moan like that again, I will bury myself inside you right now. The physician's instructions be damned." His growl reverberated through her.

Gertrude laughed, ignoring the way her body reacted to his primal statement. "We have all the time in the world."

"Correction. We have the whole world. Where would you like me to take you, *liebling*?"

"Anywhere?" Her imagination spun with possibilities.

"Preferably somewhere where no one will ever recognize us and we can be free," he added the caveat.

A picture appeared in her mind of a place she once saw in a magazine in Paris. She smiled. "I know the perfect place."

Chapter Fourteen

The *SS Friesland* stood like a sentinel in the harbor. An artic chill blasted over the water, whipping the flags back and forth. Nikolai inhaled deep letting the icy wind bite deep in his chest. Fleeting memories of his childhood and the time he served in St. Petersburg flashed through his mind. He shoved them away and pulled his wife closer, creating a protective barrier for her against the cold.

"Are you sure this is what you wish?" he whispered before pressing a kiss to her throat below her ear. "We can remain in Europe. Hide deep in the mountains of Switzerland or find an island without a soul off the coast of Greece."

"I will miss the continent, but there are so many horrible memories hidden around every corner here." She nodded firmly. "This will give us a chance to start again."

They straightened at the sight of a small cluster of people walking along the boardwalk in their direction. Nikolai recognized the countess immediately even through the layers of her ermine trimmed wool coat and hat.

"Two tickets, under a pseudonym of course, per your request. My gift to you both for years of faithful service." The countess smiled and delivered the tickets for passage. "And your wedding gift. I wish I could offer more." She retrieved a small bag from the inside pocket of her coat and deposited it in Nikolai's hand.

He opened his mouth to protest, but the countess pierced him with her most imposing glare as though daring him to reject the gracious gift. He pressed his lips together and nodded in understanding. When she set her mind to something, there was no dissuading her lest she perceive it a personal offense.

The weight settled firmly in his palm and the realization

struck him. *Gold.* He shook his head, but the countess merely grinned. He tucked the small bag into his pocket without inspecting the contents.

The countess diverted her attention to Gertrude and opened her arms in invitation. They embraced like old friends parting after a long, exhausting journey.

"Thank you for everything, Your Grace." Gertrude wiped a tear from her eye.

With a sniff, the countess waved her hand while valiantly fighting back the overwhelming emotion of the moment. "Take care of him."

"I will. I promise." Gertrude stepped aside.

There was no hesitation as the countess wrapped her arms around Nikolai.

"Be vigilant. There are still those who will question the official story with the police and try to uncover the truth of the events in the mountains." The countess whispered gripping his overcoat. "We have done our best to address it, but I cannot protect you once you leave Europe."

"I have already taken care of it." He met her bright eyes with steadfast determination. "The moment we set sail, Nikolai Voronia is dead."

The countess's lip quivered, but she recovered quickly with a shake of her head. "May he rest in peace." Passion blazed in her words. "And may you both find happiness in your new life."

"*Proshchal'nyy privet, grafinya.*" Goodbye, countess.

"*Chemú byt', togó ne minovát', milyy moy.*" *Whatever shall be, will be, darling.* With these parting words of farewell, the countess continued past them and took refuge in a carriage waiting along the street.

Nikolai took his wife's hand and smiled. "Shall we, Mrs. Zoranski?"

"Of course, Mr. Zoranski." She gripped his arm with excitement radiating around her like a golden halo. "A new world awaits us."

"I cannot think of a soul on earth I would rather explore it with, *liebling.*"

Together, they wandered the length of the dock and boarded the ship leading them to freedom and a new life.

Once the ship departed and the coast of France lay well out of sight, Nikolai took his wife in his arms and kissed her soundly. She swayed against him, clinging to his arms and heaving a breathless sigh.

"What was that for?" She grinned dazed from his amorous attentions. He loved the flush of pink on her cheeks and the soft pillows of her lips pressed into a teasing pout.

"Can I not kiss my wife?" He shrugged before he sat on the small bed in their quarters. "We have three weeks until the ship reaches New York." A million wicked ideas of how they could fill this abundance of time filled his mind.

"I do not think it is appropriate for us to spend the entire voyage locked in our quarters engaging in..." She blushed and drifted off.

"Say the word, *liebling*." He kissed her neck. "Fucking."

"Fucking." She gasped as he bit the curve of her throat.

"You are my wife now. If I want to fuck you for three weeks, then I will do it." He growled and pulled her tight against him grinding his hips against her ass. "I have waited long enough to have you in my bed. I have years to make up for this depravation." He grasped her breast in his hand and teased the nipple through the fabric.

"Nikolai," she moaned his name and the sound shot instantly to his cock. "Wait."

He paused, one hand cupping her breast, the other a breath away from the sweet warmth between her thighs. "Must you test my patience, love? I am desperate for you."

"On the docks, when you spoke with the countess," Gertrude asked, her breathing labored, "What did you mean, 'Nikolai Voronia is dead?'" she licked her lips and clarified. "I know why we changed our names and married under our new identities, but the way you said it...well, it gave me the impression you were not speaking metaphorically."

He sighed and withdrew his hands. She curled on his lap and faced him, the rose hue on her cheeks and lust in her gaze undiminished by her inopportune curiosity.

Nikolai rubbed his hand over his stubbled jaw. "The countess and I arranged an accident in which Nikolai Voronia, her trusted guard, would meet his demise." He sighed. "With him dead, no one will search for him or his past."

"It does not guarantee someone will not come looking for you or question your past." She cocked her head and rested her hand over his heart. "What will we tell those who ask about where we come from?"

"The truth, in part. We traveled Europe in the service of a noble family." He chuckled. "Most Americans will not know, nor will they care. Where we are going, there will only be wilderness as far as the eye can see."

Gertrude drew her lip between her teeth. "How exciting. I never imagined I would be on my way to America with the man I love by my side."

"Neither did I." He captured her jaw between his fingers and drew her mouth down to his.

She shifted in his lap and straddled his thighs, hoisting her skirts around her waist. Her arms draped over his shoulders as she kissed him. Her mouth intoxicated him with the sweetness of honey and her spice.

"If you keep me locked in here to fuck me every day until we reach New York City, people will talk." She gasped when he stroked along the slit in her drawers feeling her wetness coat his fingertips.

"Let them talk." He kissed her hard and unfastened his belt, shifting enough as to free his cock.

She lowered herself onto him, her head dropping back in delightful abandon. The sinful moan from her lips made him even harder.

He swore as her body clenched around him, unrelenting. "You feel like heaven."

Gertrude rocked against him, slowly grinding her hips and pumping over his cock. He captured her hips in his hands and met her movements, thrust for thrust. Her panting moans echoed in the small cabin mixing with his murmured filthy encouragements.

She adored when he spoke in Russian, in German, in English. It did not matter if she could not understand them, she knew by the way he spoke, the words were only to draw out her pleasure and brand himself to her in every way.

He found the swollen nub hidden between her folds and stroked while he raked his teeth along the bare skin of her throat.

Her hips bucked wildly against him as she found her release. Nikolai swallowed the keening cry from her lips as her cunt clenched around him in waves of ecstasy. He lost himself in the midst of her bliss and followed his own release through to conclusion, filling her with his seed and claiming her without hesitation.

She belonged to him, as he belonged to her. Nothing would come between them.

As the pleasure ebbed away, they clung to each other, their breaths hard and fast. He tipped her chin up and kissed her lips with reverence.

"Are you sure I cannot remain here and repeat this over and over until we reach New York?" He grinned, teasing her.

"If you keep it up, I shall be with child before we reach our destination."

The thought of Gertrude swollen with his seed, his child, filled him with equal amounts of trepidation and joy. She must have seen the flash of uncertainty in his eyes because she drew back and frowned.

"Do you not want children?" she asked. "I...well, I do not even know if I can have any more...after..." She dropped her gaze quickly.

Nikolai cradled her face in his hands and gently lifted her face to meet his gaze. "I would love nothing more than to have you carry my child. Our child." He licked his lips. "I never imagined I would ever want children. Honestly, I had not given it any thought before."

"Oh." She closed her eyes, hiding the hurt.

"Look at me," he pleaded. "Whether you have children or we adopt a whole pack of them, it is a pack, right?" His heart breathed a sigh of relief when she smiled. "I do not care which, so long as I have you by my side and I can fuck you every day for the rest of our lives."

She grasped his wrist and kissed it. "You truly are insatiable."

"And you love me for it, *liebling*." He winked. "You are as insatiable as I am. Minx."

Her laughter echoed through the cabin.

"Come. Let us take a walk." He gently helped her back onto her feet.

"I thought you were insatiable and never wished to leave the cabin." She teased with a grin.

"Yes, well, I plan on making the journey memorable, to be sure, but we do require sustenance. I am starving." Nikolai rubbed his stomach. "A man cannot fuck without proper replenishment."

Gertrude kissed him again. "Such a romantic."

"A realist, *liebling*." He returned the kiss with fervor. "I am a realist. You, my love, are the romantic. If it were not for your prose, we would never have reached this point."

She blushed. "Do you still have the journal that started it all?"

"I do." He grinned. "As well as the major's."

"What do you plan to do with it anyway?" She worried her lip. "You should return it."

"A dead man returns his friend's missing journal." Nikolai pondered the possibilities and an idea formulated in his mind. "Perhaps I shall. Thank you, love. You are an inspiration."

"Of course, I am." She flicked the loose edge of his cravat. "Never forget it."

"Wicked vixen. How I love you."

"I love you too. Now, let us find some food. You will need your strength later." With a wink, she opened the door and stepped out into the hall.

Nikolai whispered a prayer of thanks and let the past fall away. The future certainly looked bright ahead.

EPILOGUE

August 24, 1901
Somewhere in Wyoming

The sun beat down hot on the high plains desert. Nikolai sidestepped to the left taking refuge beneath the oversized cottonwood tree next to the barn. He leaned the shovel against the trunk and wiped the sweat from his brow with the handkerchief Gertrude made for him the prior Christmas. When he adjusted his hat into place, he scanned the horizon, a trait borne of habit.

Their forty-acre farm lay a few hours ride north of Cheyenne and a day's haul to Denver. Not that it mattered. They rarely left their farm, and what supplies they needed they ordered in their small town. The scenery changed, but the views were still spectacular. Still, the thought of the upcoming winter excited him. He preferred the bite of colder temperatures.

A figure appeared on the horizon moving along the road headed into Guernsey. Nikolai squinted, watching as the shadow approached. Not a shadow. A carriage. Who in the devil would be paying a call this time of day?

He headed toward the farmhouse where the curtains danced in the open windows and the front door stood propped open allowing the breeze to cool the heat trapped by the sun. The carriage kept a steady pace, but its course remained fixed. He hesitated before deciding against pulling the shotgun from behind the door. The pistol on his hip would work well enough.

"*Liebling*, we have guests." His voice carried from the porch onto the breeze and through the house.

Gertrude appeared in the doorway with their chubby, cherub faced daughter on her hip. "Guests?" she scanned the horizon, her eyes widening when she spotted the carriage. "Well, isn't this a pleasant surprise. Perhaps they came for Emmy's birthday." She kissed Emmy and cooed in German. Emmy shoved her tiny fist in her mouth and laughed.

Nikolai drew his pistol out of an abundance of caution. Since they left Europe, life had been blessedly quiet. No questions. No threats. Only freedom. It all seemed too good to last. Perhaps the past had finally caught up to them.

"Nikolai, put that away. You have no idea who this is and if they arrive with a gun aimed at their heads, how will it look?" She propped her hand on her free hip and glared at him. "Honestly. It is probably the reverend and his wife come to pay us a call since you refused to go to service the past month."

"It is too damn hot to sit inside." Nikolai growled and holstered his pistol begrudgingly.

"I will prepare something cold to drink." She stepped closer and handed Emmy down to him. "Here. Hold her while I fetch some refreshments."

Nikolai held Emmy in one arm and tousled her blonde curls with his free hand. The little girl stared up at him with wide jade eyes and smiled revealing four teeth.

"Da." She grabbed the handkerchief wrapped around Nikolai's neck. He grinned and kissed her forehead.

The sound of the approaching carriage drew his attention. It rattled up the road and under the arch leading to their farm. Two people occupied it. A man and a woman. Maybe Gertrude was right, maybe it was the reverend and his wife.

He shifted Emmy so he had access to his pistol should the need arise. The carriage rolled to a stop, and Nikolai narrowed his gaze as the unexpected guests stepped down from the carriage.

"That's far enough," Nikolai called out. "State your business."

"I travel halfway around the world and this is the welcome I get?" A familiar voice rang across the dusty expanse.

Elation and pride filled him. The major found his message hidden inside the journal, just as he knew he would.

"Well, I see you received your journal." Nikolai crossed to greet his guests.

"I did." Anson grinned and clasped hands firmly. His gaze fixed on Emmy and his smile widened. "Is this your daughter?"

Emmy buried her face against his chest upon seeing the major. Nikolai laughed. "Yes. Meet Emmy. She's a year old today."

"Oh, well aren't you the cutest little thing!" Matilda appeared next to the major.

"I see you two finally worked things out." Nikolai nodded to Matilda. "Mrs. Montgomery, I presume."

"Mr. Voronia, call me Matilda." She opened her arms to Emmy who eyed her with open curiosity before shaking her head. Matilda pouted playfully.

"Not Voronia anymore, Zoranski." He sighed. "It is a long story. Come, Gertrude will be pleased to see you both."

"Major Montgomery!" Gertrude called from the house. "Matilda!" She ran down the stairs and the women fell together in a fond embrace chattering instantly.

While the women fell into conversation, Nikolai turned to Anson. "You worked out the code I see."

"I nearly missed it. But you knew I would comb over every word of that journal, didn't you?" Anson laughed at Nikolai's shrug.

"I knew if anyone could find me, it would be you." He winked. "But only because I left a trail of breadcrumbs for you."

"It is good to see your humor has not changed." Anson chuckled. "Damn, it's good to see you. When I read the article in the paper about your death, I couldn't believe a word. It would take more than a runaway carriage to kill Nikolai Voronia."

"Sit down. You have come a long way." Nikolai led them to a pair of rocking chairs on the porch. He settled into the seat and sat Emmy on his lap. She gurgled contentedly tugging at the handkerchief between her chubby fists.

"I never thought I would see you become a father." Anson shook his head.

"Neither did I. What about you? Any children yet?"

"Well, actually, we just found out Matilda will be having our first."

"Congratulations."

A squeal and laughter erupted inside the house.

"It seems my wife told your wife the happy news." Anson burst into laughter.

"You did not journey all this way because of my breadcrumbs." Nikolai sensed a deeper reason behind their visit.

"No." The major raked his hand through his hair. "When I first received the journal, I wanted to hunt you down and kill you." He shrugged. "At least I did until I visited the countess who showed me the article revealing your death."

Nikolai sat quietly and listened.

"I spent months researching, traveling, and asking questions. I combed through the journal and found your coded message. I followed the clues you left for me." He sighed. "But I could not quite understand what the larger picture was. Why you faked your own death and disappeared from Europe completely? The countess refused to answer my questions, maintaining the story of your death was the truth."

"You came all this way to hear the truth from me?" Nikolai smirked.

"No. After traveling Europe for months, Matilda suggested we follow your lead and move to America. We sold everything and came west, hoping we found you in the process."

"And what if you never found me?"

"If that happened, we would continue to California. Who knows, we may still get there."

Nikolai bounced Emmy on his lap. "Not with a little one." He gestured to the east. "There's a farm a half mile east that came available a week ago. I can put a good word in for you, if you have any interest."

"I am no farmer, Nikolai. Hell, I may be too old to be a father at this point."

"If I can do both, then you can. Remember, I am older than you are."

Gertrude and Matilda reappeared with trays tall glasses of

fresh sarsaparilla.

"Ma!" Emmy reached for Gertrude, who set the tray down on the table between Anson and Nikolai.

She picked up the baby. "What are you boys talking about?"

"Just offering some advice to an old friend." Nikolai stood, allowing his wife to sit in the rocking chair.

Anson did the same. "What I really want to know is why the hell you up and disappeared without a word of warning."

"Oh, that is a long story. You may want to stay a while." Gertrude's gaze lingered on Nikolai.

"Well, we have no plans at the moment, and I could use a good story." Anson leaned on the back of his wife's chair.

Nikolai straightened and slapped his hat against his thigh. "Give me a hand in the barn while the ladies rest before supper. You are more than welcome to stay here tonight."

"No story?" Gertrude pouted.

"After supper, *liebling*, daylight is burning." Nikolai led Anson to the barn and put up his horse in an empty stall.

Later that evening after a hearty meal, the two couples sat comfortably near the hearth and talked. Gertrude rocked Emmy against her chest, nestled deep in a faded pink blanket. Matilda and Anson sat hand in hand while Nikolai recounted their version of events on the Alpine Express and beyond.

When he reached the reveal, Nikolai drew out the suspense enjoying the expression of surprise on their faces when he unmasked the villain.

"Dr. Archer?" Matilda screeched. "The one who bandaged my foot? That sweet old man?"

"Not sweet. Evil." Gertrude scowled at the memory. "Pure evil."

"But why was he after you?" Anson's brow furrowed in confusion.

"I come from a noble lineage. He discovered my true parentage and wished to kill me because of it."

"Noble? Like royalty?" Matilda asked, her curiosity piqued.

"He is the bastard son of Alexander II." Gertrude stated the fact almost nonchalantly.

Both Matilda and Anson's mouths gaped.

"Wait, the countess knew then?" Anson pinched his eyes closed at the realization. "No wonder she refused to tell me anything and why she maintained your death. She was protecting you."

"Of course," Matilda added. "It all makes perfect sense now."

"Gertrude and I decided it was best for everyone involved if we left Europe entirely. Start over somewhere new, somewhere no one would ever think to search for us."

"Except me." Anson chimed in.

"I wanted you to find us." Nikolai paused. "I never meant for our friendship to end the way I left it."

Anson blinked twice before finding a response. "Are you truly the same person? Who are you and what have you done with Nikolai?"

The four of them laughed and a peaceful camaraderie settled over the house.

Nikolai raised his whiskey in salute. "To new beginnings and past adventures on the Alpine Express."

"Hear, hear." The three responded to his toast.

Never in his life had Nikolai felt so safe and loved. His home and his heart lay wherever his family and friends resided. Nothing beyond these four walls mattered. Not anymore. He was finally where he belonged.

THE END

OTHER BOOKS BY KIRSTEN S. BLACKETER

CRAVING 1985 SERIES
When I Found You
Can't Fight This Feeling
She Gives Love a Bad Name
Owner of a Lonely Heart
Just What I Needed

HISTORICAL
An Irresistible Shadow
A Shadow's Kiss
Mississippi Moonshine
Deceiving the Earl
Jewel of Winter
At Winter's Demand
Under Winter's Control
Seducing Winter's Gentleman
Stealing the Widow's Heart
Seduction on the Alpine Express
Temptation on the Alpine Express

CONTEMPORARY
A Lockdown Love Affair
A Holiday Love Affair
Mistletoe and Mistakes
Confessions of a Fangirl
Confessions of a Gamer Girl
Confessions of a Glamour Girl
The Flight Before Christmas

FANTASY/FAIRYTALE
Curse of the Huntsman's Jewel
The Huntsman's Revenge

PIRATES AND PERSUASION
Queen Takes Hook

ABOUT THE AUTHOR
KIRSTEN S. BLACKETER

Kirsten S. Blacketer is a multi-published indie author of both historical and contemporary romance. When she's not writing, she homeschools her two children and enjoys time with her family. In those moments of freedom, she devours romance novels while sipping a glass of wine. Age has only shown her that writing villains can be just as fun as heroes. Her next life goals are to write a New York Times Bestseller and one day have Adam Driver play a starring role in a film version of one of her books. A girl can dream, right?

Read more at **http://kirstensblacketer.com.**

ALSO WRITES AS JEN BRADLEE